Were we wrong

by
Anjali Singh

Were We Wrong

Chapter One

In the quiet corners of my memory, where the echoes of laughter and the warmth of family dwell, I find the beginning of a story that has shaped my life. I am Nilu, and as I pen down these words, I invite you into the sacred spaces of my past, where reality mingles with the brushstrokes of fiction, preserving the essence while veiling identities for the sake of privacy.

As I sat with my father, a man whose eyes held the wisdom of a thousand stories, I sensed a shift in the air—a secret waiting to be shared. With a quiet grace, my father began, "Nilu, there's a chapter in your life about to unfold, one woven by the hands of tradition. Listen, my child, for destiny has its own way of writing our stories."

In the hush of that moment, he unfolded the plan orchestrated by our elders, a tapestry of arranged marriage. The name Dharamveer floated into my world, a soldier's name, a guardian standing at the borders of my unknown future. His tales resonated with honor and duty, and my heart, like a fluttering bird, danced between curiosity and apprehension.

"Baba, a soldier? How do I marry someone I've never met?" I asked, my voice a blend of curiosity and concern. His response, adorned with the pride of a father, painted Dharamveer as a man of strength and courage. The prospect of a life intertwined with someone I had yet to meet left me in a whirlwind of emotions.

As I sought solace in the comforting arms of my mother, her words were a balm to my restless heart. "Nilu, love often unfolds in the most unexpected chapters of our lives. Trust in the traditions that guide us, and let your heart navigate this uncharted journey," she whispered, her words a soothing melody in the symphony of my uncertainties.

In the company of my dearest friends, the tale of Dharamveer became the heart of our conversations. Amidst shared dreams and girlish giggles, we painted a canvas of what our futures might hold. I, caught between the threads of tradition and the dreams of a young heart, pondered the unknown with a mix of excitement and contemplation

Days turned into weeks, and anticipation hung thick in the air as we prepared for the day when Dharamveer and his family would step into our world. The prospect of meeting him, a stranger yet a significant part of my destiny, fueled a peculiar dance of emotions within me. Would he be kind? Would our hearts find harmony in the orchestrated steps of tradition?

The day arrived, marked by the aroma of sweets and the laughter of family. Dharamveer's family, led by his farmer father, entered our home, and the delicate dance of tradition and hospitality began. The elders exchanged pleasantries, and in the exchanged glances and smiles, the silent language of arranged marriages unfolded.

Rituals commenced, each step a nod to the age-old customs of a Bihari arranged marriage. Gifts were exchanged, and the courtyard echoed with the sounds of traditional music, creating a backdrop against which our destinies intertwined. Conversations with Dharamveer, cautious yet laced with the promise of a shared future, became the heartbeat of the day.

As the rituals unfolded, I found myself engaged in conversations that went beyond the surface—a glimpse into the person Dharamveer was, his dreams, and the rhythm of his heart. The Bihari customs, rich in tradition and symbolism, bound us in a sacred union, setting the stage for the chapters that awaited us.

In the midst of festivities, my heart embraced the fusion of past and future, tradition and love. Through the vibrant colors of rituals and the heartfelt exchanges with Dharamveer, I discovered the beauty in the orchestrated dance of arranged marriages. Unbeknownst to me, this union, born from tradition, would become the canvas on which our unique love story unfolded—a story that transcended the boundaries of time and tradition. And so, dear reader, with each word etched in the ink of my memories, I invite you to join me on this journey—a journey where the threads of arranged marriage wove a tale of love, destiny, and the timeless beauty of Bihari customs.

Chapter Two

In the quiet embrace of the evening, Dharamveer and I found ourselves alone, surrounded by the gentle rustle of leaves and the soft symphony of nature. The air was charged with a blend of excitement and hesitation, the unspoken dance of two souls navigating the spaces between strangers and soon-to-be companions.

As we exchanged glances, a shy smile played on our lips, the unspoken language of newfound connection. The initial moments were veiled in the fabric of hesitancy, the words cautious, and the pauses pregnant with anticipation. But gradually, as the sun dipped below the horizon, the walls of shyness crumbled, revealing the true essence of our beings.

I took a tentative step, sharing stories of my childhood, the laughter that echoed through the walls of my home. "I have one sister and three brothers," I began, the names of my siblings dancing on my tongue like cherished melodies. "Jitu, Veer, and Ghanu are my brothers, and Renu, my sister, is everyone's favorite. She's the beacon of joy in our lives, the one who binds us all with her warmth."

Dharamveer listened with an attentive gaze, the curiosity in his eyes igniting a spark of connection. I unraveled tales of my school days, the mischief with friends, and the dreams that painted the canvas of my youth. Each word echoed the love I held for my family, the cornerstone of my world.

As the moon ascended in the sky, casting its gentle glow upon us, Dharamveer's turn came to unveil the chapters of his life. His voice, a melody that resonated with sincerity and warmth, wove tales of love and loyalty. "I have three brothers—Raj, Ramu, and Rupesh," he began, the names carrying the weight of shared history. "And my three sisters— Ramya, Simmu, and Vidhya—are the pillars of our family. They're my strength, my confidantes."

His eyes sparkled as he spoke of his family, a love that transcended the boundaries of blood. "Family is everything to me," he confessed, and in those words, I felt the resonance of his heart with mine. We shared stories for hours, the tapestry of our lives weaving into a shared history that surpassed the confines of our individual narratives.

In the quietude of that evening, we exchanged more than words; we exchanged trust. It was as if the universe conspired to bring two souls together, allowing vulnerability to flourish in the shared space between us. The night, with its myriad of stars, bore witness to the birth of a connection that held the promise of enduring through time.

As we parted ways, each step felt lighter, the burden of unfamiliarity replaced by the comfort of knowing and being known. A quote I once read echoed in my mind, "Trust is built in the smallest of moments." And indeed, within the realm of those hours spent in shared tales, trust had found its place.

Dharamveer left for his home, a silhouette against the moonlit night, and in that

moment, the journey of our hearts had only just begun. Little did we know that this solitary evening, filled with laughter, stories, and the magic of connection, would become the cornerstone of a love story that defied the boundaries of time and tradition.

But in the wake of the looming demands for dowry, a cloud of tension hung over our home like a heavy monsoon rain. The notion of dowry, an age-old tradition in Bihari arranged marriages, felt like a shackle on the wings of happiness. My father, a man of principles, found himself at the crossroads of tradition and morality.

"Dowry is like an unjust tax on love," my father sighed, as we shared a quiet moment, his eyes reflecting the turmoil within. He explained the paradox—the contradiction of a practice considered normal in our culture, yet inherently wrong. "In our society, it has become the norm, Nilu. Daughters' families, caught between societal expectations and financial burdens, find themselves compelled to fulfill these demands."

As the days unfolded, we navigated the maze of societal pressure, silently shouldering the weight of expectations. The demands, extravagant and unfair, became a financial ordeal for my family.

The dowry, meant to be a gesture of love and acceptance, had transformed into a transactional burden that marred the purity of matrimonial unions.

Despite the financial strain, my father, with love in his heart and resilience in his spirit, decided to face the storm head-on. He saw the dowry demand not as a transaction, but as an opportunity to demonstrate his love for me. The sacrifices made for the sake of societal expectations became a testament to the depth of his affection.

As the wedding preparations unfolded, the unavoidable expenditures strained our resources. The paradox deepened as our community, quick to criticize the dowry system in public, indulged in it privately. It was a theater of hypocrisy, where societal norms clashed with personal beliefs, leaving families entangled in a web of judgment and expectations.

In this tempest of contradictions, I found my voice. "Dharamveer, I won't be a part of this unjust system.

Love should be the foundation of our union, not material transactions," I declared, my words fueled by a conviction to challenge the norm. Dharamveer, with a steadfast gaze, supported my stand, aligning our hearts in the face of tradition.

However, resistance faced an unyielding force in Dharamveer's father. Despite our plea for change, he remained adamant, refusing to contribute a single rupee towards the marriage expenses. In that pivotal moment, my father, standing beside me with a love that knew no bounds, stepped forward.

"It's not dowry," he asserted, a hint of defiance in his voice. "I am giving expenditure for my daughter's marriage, a celebration that involves both families. It's not a burden; it's a joy we share. Let this be an act of love, not an obligation."

The decision to shoulder the expenses became a symbol of our commitment to challenge societal norms. My father's unwavering support and refusal to bow to unjust demands were rooted in a love that transcended the materialistic expectations of a flawed tradition. In that

act, he not only protected our dignity but also laid the groundwork for change.

As the wedding day approached, my family, bound by love and trust, faced the challenges of tradition with resilience. The narrative shifted from dowry to an expression of love, transforming a seemingly burdensome ordeal into a testament to the strength of familial bonds. In the journey of challenging norms, love emerged as the guiding force, paving the way for a future where marriages could be celebrated without the shadows of societal expectations.

Chapter Three

In the quaint village of their ancestors, amidst the lush fields and swaying palms, preparations for the wedding of Nilu andDharamveer were underway. The air buzzed with excitement as relatives from near and far gathered to partake in the joyous occasion. Customs and rituals, passed down through generations, took on new meaning as the families came together to celebrate the union of two souls. From the auspicious haldi ceremony, where turmeric paste was applied to the bride and groom to cleanse and purify, to the vibrant mehendi ceremony, where intricate designs were painted onto Nilu's hands and feet as symbols of love and fertility, each ritual carried with it a sense of reverence and tradition. Narayan and Ayodhya, the patriarchs of their respective clans, took great pride in overseeing thepreparations for their children's wedding. Despite the financial burdens that often accompanied such festivities, they sparedno expense in ensuring that every detail was attended to withcare and devotion. Relatives, both near and distant, poured infrom all corners of the region, their faces aglow with smilesand laughter. But amidst the joyous festivities, there

*lingeredan undercurrent of apprehension—
a reminder of the societal expectations and
judgments that often accompanied suchoccasions.
As the sun dipped below the horizon, casting a
golden glow over the village, Nilu and
Dharamveer stood hand in hand, ready to embark
on the next chapter of theirlives together.
Surrounded by their families and loved ones,
lives together. Surrounded by their families and
loved ones, they exchanged vows of love and
commitment, their hearts overflowing with joy
and gratitude. The wedding ceremony,steeped in
tradition yet infused with modernity, served as a
testament to the power of love to transcend barriers
and unite hearts. Relatives, once divided by societal
norms, came together in a spirit of harmony and
acceptance, their differences melting away in the
warmth of Nilu and Dharamveer's love.
As the festivities continued long into the night, the village
echoed with the sounds of laughter and music, a
celebration of love in its purest form. And as Nilu and
Dharamveer made their way into the world as husband
and wife, they carried with them the blessings of their
families and the hope of a future where love would
always reign supreme.*

The next morning, the sun rose to a day filled with a
bittersweet air. It was time for Nilu's Vidai ceremony, a
poignant tradition symbolizing the bride's departure from
her parents' home to start a new life with her husband and

his family. The atmosphere was charged with emotion as Nilu, dressed in her resplendent bridal attire, prepared to bid farewell to the home and family she had known all her life.

Nilu's parents stood by, their hearts heavy with a mixture of sorrow and joy. Her mother's eyes were filled with tears, while her father held her hand, offering silent support. The ritual began with heartfelt blessings and wellwishes. Nilu touched the feet of her elders, receiving their blessings, and hugged her family members, holding onto each moment.

As Nilu stepped into the decorated car with Dharamveer by her side, her heart pounded with a mix of anticipation and anxiety. The car moved slowly through the village streets, lined with friends and well-wishers who showered them with flower petals and blessings. Nilu looked back at her parents' home, a place filled with memories, and then turned her gaze forward, towards her new life.

Upon arriving at her in-laws' house, Nilu was greeted with traditional aarti and welcomed with open arms. The house, bustling with relatives and new faces, felt overwhelming at first. Each room, each corner, was unfamiliar, and she felt the weight of adjusting to this new environment.

The first few days were challenging. Nilu found herself navigating through new customs and expectations, trying to find her place in this new household. The kitchen, where she had spent so many joyful hours with her mother, now seemed like a foreign territory. The routines and rituals were different, and she missed the comfort of her old home.

However, through it all, Dharamveer remained her unwavering support. He sensed her struggles and was always there with a comforting word or a reassuring smile. He introduced her to his family's traditions with patience and understanding, making sure she never felt alone. He took her on walks through their village, sharing stories of his childhood, and gradually, Nilu began to feel a connection to her new surroundings.

Dharamveer's mother, too, played a crucial role in Nilu's adjustment. She treated Nilu with kindness and respect, guiding her through the intricacies of her new household. Nilu's gentle demeanor and willingness to learn endeared her to her new family. Slowly but surely, she began to find joy in her new roles and responsibilities.

Nilu's evenings were filled with the warmth of family gatherings, and she discovered new friendships among her sisters-in-law and neighbors. She started contributing her own touches to the household, blending the traditions she brought with her with those of her new family. She found solace in small moments – cooking a meal that reminded her of home, sharing stories with her new relatives, and experiencing the love and support of her husband.

As weeks turned into months, Nilu realized that she had not only adapted to her new life but had also enriched it with her presence. The home that once felt unfamiliar now resonated with her laughter and love. Nilu and Dharamveer, together, built a life where their love grew stronger with each passing day. With each challenge they faced, their bond deepened, and they became each other's greatest strength.

In the heart of the village, surrounded by family and friends, Nilu and Dharamveer's love story continued to blossom, a testament to the enduring power of love and the beauty of new beginnings

Chapter Four

After Nilu and Dharamveer spent some cherished time together, it was soon time for Dharamveer to return to his duty. He was posted in Jammu and Kashmir, a region known for its beauty as well as its challenges. The day of his departure arrived, casting a shadow over the newfound joy in their lives.

The morning was filled with an uneasy silence. Nilu watched as Dharamveer packed his belongings, her heart heavy with the impending separation. They shared a quiet breakfast, and every glance, every touch, was a silent promise of their love and strength. As Dharamveer prepared to leave, Nilu held back her tears, wanting to be strong for him. He hugged her tightly, whispering words of comfort and assurance, and with a final kiss, he was gone.

The first few days after Dharamveer's departure were the hardest. The house felt empty, and every corner reminded Nilu of him. She went about her daily chores with a sense of numbness, her mind constantly drifting to thoughts of him. The bed felt too large, the evenings too quiet, and her heart ached with longing.

Nilu tried to keep herself busy, immersing herself in household tasks and helping her mother-in-law with daily responsibilities. She found solace in the small routines, in cooking meals, and tending to the garden. Yet, the nights were the loneliest. She would lie awake, staring at the ceiling, replaying memories of their time together, and wishing for his safe return.

Letters became their lifeline. Every word Dharamveer wrote was a balm to her aching heart. She would read and reread his letters, finding comfort in his written words. In her replies, she poured out her heart, sharing her days and expressing her love and longing. Each letter was a piece of him, and she cherished them dearly.

Nilu also found strength in her faith and the support of her family. Her motherin-law, understanding her pain, would often sit with her, sharing stories of her own experiences and offering words of wisdom and comfort. The bond between them grew stronger, and Nilu began to feel a deeper sense of belonging in her new family.

Despite the challenges, Nilu discovered her own resilience. She learned to navigate the village on her own, handling responsibilities that she had never faced before. She managed finances, dealt with household repairs, and even took part in community events. Each accomplishment, no matter how small, was a testament to her strength and adaptability.

As the seasons changed, so did Nilu. She found a quiet strength within herself, fueled by the love she shared with Dharamveer. She missed him deeply, every day, but she also knew that their love transcended the physical distance. She carried him in her heart, and that gave her the courage to face each day with hope.

Nilu's letters to Dharamveer were filled with stories of her daily life, her triumphs, and her struggles. She shared her dreams and fears, and through this exchange, their bond only deepened. Dharamveer's words of encouragement and love were her guiding light, and she held onto them through the toughest days.

Months passed, and Nilu continued to grow in her new role. She found joy in small moments, in the laughter of children, in the beauty of a sunset, in the warmth of family gatherings. She realized that she was not alone; she was surrounded by love and support. Her love for Dharamveer gave her the strength to endure and the hope for a brighter future.

And so, Nilu waited, with patience and faith, for the day when Dharamveer would return. She knew that their love, tested by distance and time, would emerge even stronger. In the quiet moments of her day, she would close her eyes and imagine the day he would walk through the door, and they would be reunited, their love shining brighter than ever

Time seemed to slow as Nilu awaited Dharamveer's return. Each day blended into the next, marked by routines and the subtle changes of the seasons. The village buzzed with its usual activities, but for Nilu, life felt like it was moving in slow motion. Despite her daily tasks, her thoughts constantly returned to Dharamveer, and the longing in her heart never subsided.

Life as an army man's wife was a journey of endurance and patience. Nilu faced both admiration and scrutiny from the village. Some people respected her resilience and the sacrifice she and Dharamveer were making. They often said, "It takes a strong woman to support a man on the front lines." Others, however, offered unsolicited advice and comments that sometimes felt like veiled criticisms. "It must be hard living without your husband," they would say, or "How do you manage all alone?"

Nilu learned to navigate these societal pressures with grace. She found comfort in the friendships she forged with other army wives, who understood her struggles and offered genuine support. Together, they shared their fears, hopes, and the small victories of everyday life.

Dharamveer, too, faced his own set of challenges. Fellow soldiers often spoke of the strength required to leave their families behind. "We fight for our country, but our wives fight a different battle back home," they would say during their conversations. Dharamveer's thoughts frequently turned to Nilu, and the distance made their love grow even stronger. He often wondered how she managed the responsibilities of their home and how she dealt with the social dynamics of the village.

The letters they exchanged became their lifeline, a testament to their unwavering bond. Nilu wrote her letters with care, describing the minutiae of her days and the emotions she felt. She shared stories of her achievements, her challenges, and the warmth of the village community. Each letter was a piece of her heart, and she sent them with prayers for Dharamveer's safety.

Dharamveer's letters, filled with love and reassurance, arrived sporadically. He described the camaraderie among the soldiers, the beauty of the mountains, and his longing to return home. "Every moment away from you strengthens my resolve to serve our country, but it also makes me appreciate the love we share even more," he wrote in one letter.

Their correspondence was not without its challenges. The letters often took weeks to arrive, and the wait was agonizing. Yet, each letter brought immense joy and relief, a tangible connection that bridged the miles between them. They devised ways to keep their spirits high, sharing favorite poems, jokes, and even simple sketches to lighten the mood.

Months turned into years, and Nilu's strength became a source of inspiration for many in the village. She carried on with determination, knowing that every sacrifice was for the love she and Dharamveer shared. The support of her family, the understanding of her fellow army wives, and the love in Dharamveer's letters sustained her through the toughest times.

Finally, after what felt like an eternity, the day came when an army vehicle pulled up in front of Nilu's home. Her heart raced as she saw Dharamveer step out, his uniform a reminder of his service and sacrifice. Tears of joy and relief streamed down her face as she ran into his arms, the world around them fading into a blur.

The village gathered to welcome Dharamveer home, their admiration for him evident in their eyes. "You are a hero, Dharamveer," they said, "and Nilu, your strength has been remarkable." The respect they received from the community was overwhelming, and it filled their hearts with pride.

Nilu and Dharamveer's reunion was filled with laughter, tears, and stories of the time they spent apart. They held each other close, grateful for the love that had sustained them through the distance. Together, they navigated the challenges and joys of life, knowing that their love could withstand any test.

Their journey was a testament to the resilience and strength of army families, and their story inspired many in the village. As they looked towards the future, Nilu and Dharamveer knew that whatever came their way, they would face it together, their love as their guiding light.

During the times when occasions and festivals came around, Nilu often found herself enveloped in a deep sense of longing. The vibrant colors, the joyful songs, and the festive foods that once brought her immense joy now felt incomplete without Dharamveer by her side. Diwali lights seemed dimmer, Holi colors less vibrant, and even the village's local fairs lacked their usual charm. She tried to immerse herself in the celebrations, but her thoughts always drifted to him.

She would watch other couples and families enjoying the festivities, a pang of sadness in her heart. The laughter and joy around her were a stark contrast to the emptiness she felt. The rituals and traditions, which she had always cherished, now served as constant reminders of Dharamveer's absence. She decorated the house, cooked his favorite dishes, and participated in the village gatherings, but a part of her heart was always waiting for his return.

Despite the loneliness, Nilu never allowed herself to lose hope. She knew that Dharamveer was out there, thinking of her just as much as she was thinking of him. She kept herself busy with preparations, knowing that when he finally came home, they would celebrate with double the joy to make up for lost time.

For Dharamveer, the time away from Nilu was equally difficult. The festivals and celebrations at his post were muted, the camaraderie among soldiers a small solace.

He missed the warmth of home, the sound of Nilu's laughter, and the comfort of her presence. His thoughts often wandered to her during these times, and he wondered how she was coping with the festivities alone.

An army man's salary was modest, with Dharamveer earning only 4000 rupees. Despite this, he was determined to provide for his family and ensure they lacked nothing. "Our sacrifices are the foundation of our family's future," he would often remind himself. The limited income meant careful budgeting and sacrifices, but Dharamveer approached it with the same determination he applied to his duties.

Every month, he would set aside a portion of his salary for essential expenses, making sure to send money home to Nilu. He thought of innovative ways to stretch their finances, prioritizing their needs and planning meticulously. He knew that material wealth was not the essence of a happy life; it was the love and support they shared that truly mattered.

When Dharamveer came home, it felt like all the festivals arrived at once for Nilu. His presence filled the house with an indescribable joy, making up for all the lonely times. The air felt lighter, and every small activity turned into a celebration. They would light extra lamps during Diwali, paint the village in brighter colors during Holi, and sing louder songs during local fairs. Their reunion was a festival in itself, one that radiated love and happiness.

Dharamveer brought small gifts for Nilu, tokens of his love and remembrance, bought with the little he could save. "It's not about how much we have, but how much we cherish what we have," he would say, handing her a simple but meaningful gift. These gestures, though modest, were priceless to Nilu, who cherished each one as a symbol of their enduring love.

The villagers admired Nilu's strength and Dharamveer's dedication. They would say, "Nilu, you are the embodiment of patience and love," and to Dharamveer, "Your service and sacrifices are the pillars of our safety and freedom." The respect and admiration from the community were heartwarming and a testament to their resilience.

Together, Nilu and Dharamveer built a life where love was the true wealth. They faced challenges with courage and celebrated every moment they had together. Their story was a beacon of hope and strength, showing that with love, even the toughest times could be endured and that true happiness came from the heart, not material wealth .

Chapter Five

Despite the deep love and strong bond between Nilu and Dharamveer, life in his absence was far from easy. The responsibility of managing the household fell heavily on Nilu's shoulders, and the dynamics within the family made her situation even more challenging.

Dharamveer's unmarried sister, Ramya, was a spirited young woman with little interest in household chores. She spent most of her time focusing on her studies and socializing with friends. While Nilu understood Ramya's priorities, the lack of support from her sister-in-law added to her burden. Often, Nilu would wake up early to prepare breakfast and begin her daily chores, only to see Ramya leisurely enjoying her time. "Ramya, could you please help me with the dishes?" Nilu would ask gently, hoping for some assistance. Ramya's response was usually dismissive, "I have to study, Bhabhi. I'll do it later." But later never came, and the pile of chores remained Nilu's responsibility.

The situation was compounded by the presence of Dharamveer's elder brother's wife, Suman. Suman was a strict and domineering woman who believed in traditional hierarchies within the household. She often scolded Nilu and imposed an unfair share of work on her. "Nilu, make sure the floors are spotless," Suman would command, her tone leaving no room for refusal. "And don't forget to wash the clothes and prepare dinner on time. You are the newest member here; it's your duty to maintain the house."

Nilu's day was a relentless cycle of cleaning, cooking, and attending to every small need of the family. She swept and mopped the floors, washed the laundry, cooked meals, and even tended to the garden. Her own aspirations and moments of rest were put on hold as she worked tirelessly to meet the demands of her inlaws. The festive occasions, which should have brought joy, often meant even more work. "Nilu, make sure the house is perfectly decorated for Diwali," Suman would order, adding to her already heavy workload.

Nilu's hands were often chapped from constant washing, and her back ached from hours of bending and lifting. Despite her exhaustion, she rarely received any appreciation. Instead, criticism was frequent. If something wasn't up to Suman's standards, Nilu would hear about it. "Why is this corner still dirty? Can't you do anything right?" Suman would snap, making Nilu feel inadequate and disheartened.

The emotional toll was significant. Nilu missed Dharamveer deeply and longed for his presence, not just for companionship but for the balance he brought to her life. His letters, filled with love and encouragement, were her only solace. "I miss you so much, Nilu. I know it's hard, but please stay strong. Our love will see us through," he would write, his words a reminder of the life and love they were fighting for.

Nilu found strength in her love for Dharamveer and her determination to honor his sacrifice. She maintained her duties with grace, often reminding herself that her efforts were a testament to her resilience. She sought small moments of peace, like a quiet cup of tea in the early morning or a brief walk in the garden. These moments were her sanctuary, a time to recharge and find solace.

Despite the harsh treatment, Nilu never let bitterness take root in her heart. She treated Ramya with kindness and tried to understand her youthful indifference. "Ramya, I know you are busy, but we are a family, and we need to support each other," Nilu would say gently, hoping to inspire some change. She also handled Suman's harshness with patience, acknowledging that tradition and societal expectations often shaped her sister-in-law's behavior.

Nilu's quiet strength did not go unnoticed by everyone. There were moments when Dharamveer's mother would offer a kind word or a small gesture of support. "You are doing well, Nilu. Keep your spirit strong," she would say, her eyes reflecting a mix of sympathy and understanding. These rare moments of acknowledgment were a balm to Nilu's weary soul.

Through all the hardship, Nilu remained resolute, her love for Dharamveer and her inner strength guiding her through each day. She believed in the power of love and hoped for a future where she and Dharamveer could build a life filled with mutual respect and joy, free from the burdens that currently weighed her down. Until then, she persevered, embodying the true spirit of resilience and love

Nilu's life at her in-laws' house was a series of silent sacrifices and unacknowledged efforts. While she continued to work tirelessly, maintaining the household and fulfilling every duty expected of her, a deeper tragedy added to her burdens.

Ramya's wedding was approaching, and preparations were in full swing. The house buzzed with excitement, and everyone seemed to be involved in the arrangements. However, as the wedding day neared, it became clear that some essential items were still needed. In a decision that was made without consulting Nilu, her in-laws decided to give away the items from Nilu's tilak ceremony to Ramya.

The tilak ceremony items held deep sentimental value for Nilu. They were gifts from her father, symbols of his love and blessings for her new life. These included intricately designed wooden furniture, decorative pieces, and other valuable items. But, in this family, decisions were often made without her consent. "We will give Nilu's tilak items to Ramya. She needs them more now," Suman declared, her tone leaving no room for discussion.

Nilu watched in silence as the items were taken away. Her heart ached, but she didn't voice her pain. She had always been taught to respect her elders and maintain harmony, even at the cost of her own happiness. "It's for Ramya's happiness," she reminded herself, forcing a smile when Ramya received the items with delight.

However, the loss of these items was a significant emotional blow to Nilu. Each piece represented her father's love and the memories of her wedding day. The sofa and bed, which were the only items left untouched, seemed to mock her silent suffering. She felt invisible, her feelings and consent disregarded entirely.

In contrast, Dharamveer had spared no expense for Ramya's wedding, ensuring that it was a grand affair. He sent money from his modest salary, making sacrifices to ensure his sister's special day was perfect. "I want Ramya's wedding to be memorable," he had written to his family, unaware of the sacrifices Nilu was being forced to make back home.

The disparity in treatment was stark. Nilu's contributions and sacrifices went unnoticed, while Ramya's wedding preparations were celebrated with enthusiasm and fanfare. Nilu's silent pain and her uncomplaining nature only added to her sense of isolation. The villagers noticed but were often silent, bound by traditional norms and the fear of causing a rift.

The day of Ramya's wedding was a whirlwind of activities. Nilu, despite her sadness, worked diligently to ensure everything went smoothly. She cooked, cleaned, and managed the guests, her tired hands and aching back bearing witness to her relentless efforts. Suman's demands were unending, and Nilu complied without a word of protest. "Nilu, make sure the guests are comfortable," Suman instructed sharply. "And don't forget to check on the arrangements in the kitchen."

Despite everything, Nilu put on a brave face. She smiled through the ceremonies, her heart heavy with the weight of her unvoiced sorrow. The joy and laughter around her felt distant, as if she were an outsider looking in. She found solace in the brief moments when she could steal away to a quiet corner, allowing herself a few moments of tears before returning to her duties.

Nilu's resilience and strength were remarkable. She never let bitterness take root in her heart, even when her own needs and desires were overlooked. She continued to fulfill her responsibilities with grace, hoping that her love and dedication would one day be acknowledged.

When Dharamveer returned home after Ramya's wedding, he sensed the underlying sadness in Nilu's eyes. She tried to hide it, but her husband knew her too well. "Is everything alright, Nilu?" he asked gently, his concern evident.

Nilu hesitated, not wanting to burden him with her troubles. But eventually, she shared her feelings, her voice trembling with suppressed emotions. "They took all the items from my tilak ceremony, Dharamveer. I didn't want to say anything, but it hurt because they were from my father," she confessed, her eyes welling up with tears.

Dharamveer's heart ached for his wife. He held her close, understanding the depth of her pain. "I'm so sorry, Nilu. I didn't know," he said softly, his voice filled with regret. "I'll make sure this never happens again. You deserve to be treated with respect and love."

Nilu's silent endurance and unwavering love for Dharamveer shone through, even in the face of adversity. She hoped that, with time, the family would recognize her sacrifices and treat her with the respect and consideration she deserved. Until then, she found strength in her love for Dharamveer and the hope for a better future together.

Chapter Six

Dharamveer's father, Kedarnath, was a man of complex character. While he had moments of kindness and wisdom, his reputation in the village was marred by his often harsh and selfish behavior. Known for his "villain acts," Kedarnath was a formidable figure who commanded respect and fear in equal measure.

Despite being a good man at heart, Kedarnath's actions often painted a different picture. He was known for his rigid discipline and unyielding nature. This extended to his relationship with Dharamveer, who faced the challenge of balancing his duty to his country with the demands of his father.

Kedarnath had a peculiar way of showing his authority. Whenever Dharamveer came home on leave, the first thing his father would ask was not about his wellbeing or his experiences on the front lines. Instead, it was always about money. "How much have you brought this time?" Kedarnath would demand, his eyes sharp and expectant.

For Dharamveer, this was a constant source of pain. An army man's life was already fraught with challenges, but having a father who prioritized money over emotional support made it even harder. Every leave, instead of a warm welcome, Dharamveer faced this cold, transactional greeting. He would hand over a significant portion of his modest salary, hoping it would please his father. "Here, Baba, I've brought 3000 rupees this time," he would say, suppressing the disappointment in his voice.

Despite this, Dharamveer never let bitterness consume him. He understood that Kedarnath's behavior stemmed from a different era and mindset. Instead of resenting his father, he chose to fulfill his duties with even more dedication. He continued to send money home regularly, knowing that it was not just a matter of respect but also a way to ensure the family's well-being.

In addition to his financial contributions, Dharamveer went to great lengths to secure his family's future. He bought fields in his father's name, hoping this would bring pride and happiness to Kedarnath. "I've bought some land, Baba. It's in your name. You can manage it as you see fit," Dharamveer informed his father, hoping to see a flicker of appreciation in his eyes.

But even these efforts seemed to fall short. Kedarnath accepted the deeds without much acknowledgment, his stern demeanor unchanged. "Good. This land will be useful," was all he said, the lack of warmth in his response a sharp contrast to Dharamveer's expectations.

For Nilu, witnessing this dynamic was heartbreaking. She saw how hard Dharamveer worked, both in the army and for his family, and how little recognition he received from his father. "You do so much for them, Dharamveer. I wish Baba could see and appreciate your efforts," she would say, her voice filled with empathy.

Dharamveer would smile, his love for Nilu and his sense of duty giving him strength. "It's okay, Nilu. Baba has his ways. I can't change that, but I can make sure I do my part. For us, for our family," he would reply, his resolve unwavering.

Despite the lack of support and recognition from Kedarnath, Dharamveer remained committed to his family. His actions were driven by love and responsibility rather than the need for approval. He believed in doing what was right, even if it meant facing constant challenges and emotional turmoil.

Kedarnath's attitude didn't go unnoticed in the village. People often talked about his sternness and the way he treated Dharamveer. "It's hard for an army man, serving the country and dealing with such a demanding father," the villagers would say. They admired Dharamveer's perseverance and the dignity with which he handled his father's demands.

Over time, Nilu and Dharamveer found solace in each other's support. They knew that life was not always fair, but their love and mutual respect made them stronger. Nilu's unwavering support and Dharamveer's steadfast commitment to his family became their pillars of strength. Together, they faced the challenges posed by Kedarnath's behavior, knowing that their love and determination would see them through.

As Dharamveer's life as an army man was a testament to his unwavering dedication and the sacrifices he made for his family. Despite being stationed far from home, his commitment to providing for and supporting his loved ones was unyielding. His story was one of relentless effort, love, and resilience.

Every day, Dharamveer woke up with a singular focus to serve his country and make his family proud. The harsh terrains and demanding duties of army life were nothing compared to the emotional weight of being separated from his family. His heart ached for his wife, Nilu, and his parents, Kedarnath and Meera, along with his younger siblings—two brothers and a sister—who looked up to him with hope and admiration.

When Dharamveer received his modest salary, he was acutely aware of the many demands on his finances. Each month, a significant portion was sent home to his father, Kedarnath, who, despite his demanding nature, was still a figure of respect. "Here's the money I promised, Baba," Dharamveer would say, handing over the cash during his rare visits home. He hoped that by fulfilling his father's financial expectations, he could bring some sense of stability to his family.

The money he sent was not just for his father. Dharamveer also allocated funds to cover the household expenses, including groceries and other necessities. During his leave, he made it a point to bring fresh vegetables and other provisions from the nearby markets. "I've got these for you, Ma. I know how much you like these vegetables," he would say, placing the bags on the kitchen counter with a tired but proud smile.

Even though his visits home were infrequent, Dharamveer never forgot to bring gifts for his entire family. He would save a portion of his salary to buy presents, ranging from small trinkets to more meaningful items. "This is for you, Nilu," he would say, handing her a carefully chosen gift. "And these are for the kids," he'd add, distributing the presents among his younger siblings. His eyes would light up with joy as he watched their faces brighten with each gift.

Dharamveer's dedication extended beyond financial support. He made sure that Nilu, who managed the household alone, received special items to ease her daily chores. He would bring back supplies that she needed, often requesting her to make a list of what was required. "I've got the groceries you wanted and a few things for the house," he would say, ensuring she had everything she needed to maintain their home.

His commitment didn't stop there. Dharamveer also worked hard to save a little for his own future and that of his family. He knew the importance of financial stability and the need to plan for unforeseen circumstances. Balancing his budget was a skill he perfected, making sure that every penny was accounted for and directed toward the well-being of his family.

In addition to managing finances, Dharamveer spent his free time writing letters to Nilu, his mother, and his siblings. These letters were filled with love, encouragement, and updates from his life on the front lines. "I miss you all dearly," he would write. "I am doing well, and I hope to return home soon to be with you."

Despite the physical distance and emotional strain, Dharamveer's dedication never wavered. His life was a continuous balancing act, juggling the demands of his military service with the responsibilities of providing for his family. Each month, he endured the loneliness of separation, fueled by the knowledge that his sacrifices were ensuring a better life for those he loved.

The villagers spoke of Dharamveer's devotion with admiration. "He's an exemplary soldier and a loving family man," they would say. "His sacrifices are the backbone of his family's well-being." They respected him not just for his service to the nation but for the way he prioritized his family despite the numerous challenges.

His commitment to serving his country and his family was a testament to his character. Every challenge he faced, every sacrifice he made, was driven by a deep love for his family and a desire to provide them with everything they needed. His life was a constant reminder that true strength lies in the ability to persevere through hardships and maintain one's commitment to loved ones, no matter how great the distance or how difficult the circumstances.

Dharamveer's life was a mosaic of sacrifice, love, and unyielding dedication. While he toiled diligently on the front lines, ensuring the safety and well-being of his family and his nation, he often faced a profound lack of emotional support from those he cared for the most.

Despite the distance and the demands of his military service, Dharamveer never failed to send money home. Each month, he meticulously calculated his budget to ensure that his father, Kedarnath, his wife, Nilu, and his siblings received what they needed. He sent home a portion of his salary, bought gifts during his rare visits, and made sure to bring fresh supplies to help Nilu manage the household. His commitment was unwavering, driven by a deep sense of duty and love for his family.

Yet, the emotional toll of his sacrifices was compounded by a painful reality: his family rarely reached out to him with genuine concern. Whenever Dharamveer received a call from home, it was often accompanied by complaints or requests for more money. The conversations were seldom about his wellbeing or how he was coping with the rigors of army life.

"Dharamveer, we need more money this month," Kedarnath would say during their phone calls. "The expenses have increased. Can you send more?"

Even when Dharamveer was unwell or facing difficulties, his family's concern was minimal. There were no comforting words or inquiries about his health. "Is the money on its way?" was the most common question, overshadowing any concern for his condition.

The emotional support that Dharamveer yearned for was notably absent. His letters were filled with updates about his life, a semblance of connection that he clung to with hope. "I'm doing alright, just a bit tired," he would write, attempting to reassure his loved ones and himself. "How is everyone at home?" In response, he often received brief replies focused on logistics rather than empathy. "We received the money, but we need more for repairs. Also, when will you be home again?" These responses left Dharamveer feeling disconnected and unappreciated, his sacrifices seemingly taken for granted.

The loneliness of army life was compounded by the absence of heartfelt communication. Dharamveer wished for a call that simply asked, "How are you? Are you eating well? Is everything okay there?" Instead, the focus remained on financial support and material needs.

Despite this emotional isolation, Dharamveer never wavered in his commitment. He continued to fulfill his responsibilities, both as a soldier and as a provider. His letters remained filled with warmth and love, a stark contrast to the transactional nature of the conversations he received in return.

Whenever he returned home on leave, he faced the same routine—giving money, bringing gifts, and fulfilling the expectations of his family. Each visit, he was met with the same requests and complaints, the emotional void everpresent.

Through it all, Dharamveer's dedication never faltered. He remained steadfast in his role, driven by a sense of duty and an unwavering love for his family. His sacrifices were a testament to his strength and resilience, despite

the lack of emotional support from those he cared for
deeply.

Chapter Seven

The passage of time brought both challenges and joys into Dharamveer and Nilu's lives. Amidst the trials and tribulations of army life and familial responsibilities, a new chapter unfolded when Nilu and Dharamveer welcomed their first child, a baby boy named Gopi.

Gopi's arrival marked a profound change in their lives. His birth took place while Nilu was staying at her mother's house, a period of support and comfort during the final days of her pregnancy. The day Gopi was born was filled with an overwhelming sense of joy and relief. The arrival of their son was a beacon of hope and happiness, bringing light into their lives amid the ongoing challenges.

Nilu cherished every moment of Gopi's early years, capturing each milestone with photographs and memories. She often reflected on the special moments of his childhood with a mixture of nostalgia and gratitude. "Look at these photos, Dharamveer," she would say, her eyes shining with pride. "Gopi's first steps, his first birthday—these are the moments I hold dear."

Nilu's words held a deeper meaning when she compared her experiences to her past visits to her in-laws' home. "If Gopi were at Baba's house, no one would bother to bring a camera to capture these precious moments," she would say with a touch of sadness. Her tone revealed the contrast between the warmth and attentiveness she experienced at her mother's home versus the distant, transactional nature of her in-laws' home.

The memories of Gopi's childhood were a testament to the love and joy that filled their lives. Nilu reminisced about the small joys—Gopi's first smile, his playful antics, and the warmth of his tiny hand in hers. "We have so many beautiful photos," she would say, "and they are not just pictures but memories of our happiness as parents."

Dharamveer's occasional visits home became even more precious with the arrival of their son. Though his time with Gopi was limited due to his duties, each visit was filled with joy. He would hold his son close, his heart swelling with pride and love. "I miss so much while I'm away," he would say, "but every moment I get to spend with Gopi is a treasure."

Despite the challenges of balancing his military duties with his responsibilities as a father, Dharamveer and Nilu worked hard to create a loving and nurturing environment for Gopi. Their love for their son was evident in the way they cared for him, ensuring he had a happy and secure childhood.

The photos of Gopi's early years became a cherished collection, a visual diary of their journey as parents. Nilu would often look at these pictures and reflect on the happiness and fulfillment they brought into their lives. "These moments are what make everything worthwhile," she would say, her voice filled with emotion.

The arrival of Gopi was a bright spot in the midst of their struggles. His laughter and innocence brought joy and a renewed sense of purpose to their lives. Nilu and Dharamveer embraced parenthood with all their hearts, finding solace and strength in the love they shared for their son.

As Gopi grew, he became the center of their world, a living testament to their love and dedication. Despite the difficulties and sacrifices they faced, the presence of their son was a constant reminder of the beauty and joy that life could offer. Nilu and Dharamveer's journey as parents was a powerful affirmation of their enduring love and commitment to each other and their family

Before Nilu went to her mother's house for the first time after her marriage, a significant family tradition and a test of goodwill came into play. According to custom, it was expected that when a bride visits her maternal home after marriage, her in-laws would send gifts, including clothes and sweets, for her entire family. This gesture was meant to show respect and maintain the familial bond between the bride's and groom's families.

However, this tradition became a source of tension and disappointment for Nilu. When her brother visited her in-laws' home to took her sister back home with him, he was met with reluctance and excuses. Kedarnath, Nilu's father-in-law, who was known for his rigid and often unsympathetic demeanor, refused to provide the customary items.

"I'm sorry, but we don't have the money for that," Kedarnath said dismissively, despite the fact that he had sufficient means. His refusal was not due to financial constraints but rather a display of stubbornness and unwillingness to follow the tradition.

Nilu was deeply hurt by this refusal. It was not just about the gifts but also about the lack of respect for the family traditions that mattered to her. Her anticipation of the visit to her mother's house was marred by this disappointment. She could only hope that things would change before she was able to leave.

Weeks passed, and Nilu's frustration grew. She felt trapped between her desire to adhere to her cultural practices and the harsh reality of her in-laws' indifference. Her longing to visit her family and present them with the customary gifts remained unfulfilled.

The situation began to change when Dharamveer returned home on leave. He was aware of the situation and the emotional strain it had caused Nilu.
Determined to make things right, Dharamveer took it upon himself to rectify the situation.

"I'm sorry for what happened earlier, Nilu," Dharamveer said when he arrived home. "I know how important this tradition is to you. I'm going to make sure we send the gifts and sweets to your family."

With resolve, Dharamveer went out to purchase the clothes and sweets, fulfilling the tradition that had been neglected. He carefully selected items to ensure they met the expectations of the customary gifts. "I want everything to be perfect," he said, his determination evident in his actions.

When the gifts were finally sent to Nilu's family, it was a moment of relief and satisfaction for her. The package, filled with clothes and sweets, was received with joy and appreciation by her family. "Look at these, Ma. Dharamveer made sure we got everything," Nilu said, her voice filled with gratitude.

The successful delivery of the gifts allowed Nilu to visit her mother's house with a sense of completeness. The visit, which had been tainted by earlier disappointments, was now a source of joy and fulfillment. Nilu was able to reconnect with her family, share the news of her life with them, and present the gifts that symbolized the bond between her family and her in-laws.

The experience highlighted Dharamveer's dedication and love for Nilu. Even in the face of his father's reluctance, he stood by his wife and upheld the traditions that mattered to her. His actions were a testament to his commitment to their marriage and his respect for Nilu's cultural values.

Chapter Eight

A few months after Nilu's visit to her mother's house, another chapter of sorrow unfolded in Dharamveer's life. His mother, Meera, who had long been in the habit of inhaling bidi, fell gravely ill. Her condition deteriorated

rapidly, and despite all efforts, she succumbed to a severe
fever.

The news of his mother's illness reached Dharamveer
while he was stationed far from home. The helplessness
of not being there during her final days weighed heavily
on him. He arranged for immediate leave, but the journey
back home seemed endless as his mind raced with worry
and sorrow.

Upon his arrival, Dharamveer found his home shrouded
in grief. The once vibrant household now echoed with the
muffled cries of mourning. Nilu was by his side, offering
silent support as he faced one of the hardest moments of
his life. "She fought hard, Dharamveer," Nilu said softly,
her eyes filled with tears. "But in the end, she couldn't
hold on."

The days that followed were a blur of rituals and
responsibilities. Dharamveer had to take charge of all the
arrangements for his mother's last rites. There was little
time to process his own grief as he managed the
multitude of tasks that needed his attention. The expenses
were substantial, but Dharamveer spared no cost to
ensure his mother received a proper farewell.

"We need to arrange for the pyre, the rituals, and the
feast," he said, coordinating with relatives and villagers.
"Everything must be done according to tradition."

As the family gathered for the funeral, Dharamveer's sorrow was compounded by the realization of how much he had missed while serving far away. His mother's passing was not just a loss of a parent but also a stark reminder of the sacrifices he made as an army man, often missing out on family moments both joyful and sorrowful.

The funeral procession was a solemn affair. Villagers joined the family, offering their condolences and support. Dharamveer led the procession, his heart heavy with the weight of loss. The sight of the pyre brought an overwhelming wave of emotion. "Rest in peace, Ma," he whispered, as he performed the final rites.

In the days that followed, Dharamveer continued to manage the aftermath of his mother's passing. The expenses for the rituals and the feast, held in her honor, added up. "We have to ensure everything is taken care of properly," he told Nilu, who stood by him throughout, providing comfort and assistance.

Despite the strain on their finances, Dharamveer ensured that no expense was spared. He knew that honoring his mother's memory was of utmost importance. The family gathered to mourn, share stories, and remember Meera's life. Each ritual, each prayer was a step towards healing, though the pain of loss remained deep.

Nilu, while mourning the loss of her mother-in-law, also played a crucial role in supporting Dharamveer. She handled the household chores and took care of Gopi, allowing Dharamveer to focus on the funeral arrangements. Her presence was a source of strength for him during this challenging time.

As the days turned into weeks, the immediate sorrow began to ebb, replaced by a quieter, lingering grief. Dharamveer found solace in his memories of his mother and the knowledge that he had done everything he could to honor her in death. "She knew you loved her, Dharamveer," Nilu would say, offering him comfort.

In the quiet moments, Dharamveer reflected on the impermanence of life and the sacrifices his family had made. He resolved to cherish the time he had with Nilu and Gopi, knowing all too well the unpredictability of his own life as an army man. His mother's passing was a stark reminder of the importance of family and the need to balance duty with personal connections.

Dharamveer's dedication to his family remained unwavering. The loss of his mother was a profound sorrow, but it also strengthened his resolve to provide for and protect his loved ones. Despite the challenges and the emotional toll, he continued to serve his country with honor, driven by the love and memories of those he held dear.

Dharamveer's life was marked by responsibility and sacrifice, not just for his country but also for his family. His elder brother, Ramu, had his own role to play in the family dynamics, particularly in the initial years of Dharamveer's marriage.

Before joining the military, Dharamveer managed the family's grocery shop in Bahaya, a small town where Kedarnath, their father, had inherited some property. This shop was a significant source of income for the family. When Dharamveer left for the army, Ramu stepped in to take over the business. The transition was essential, as the younger brothers were still children and unable to contribute financially.

Despite Ramu taking over the grocery shop, he showed little concern for the overall well-being of the family. His focus remained on the business, and he often neglected the financial needs of the household. This attitude left a considerable burden on Dharamveer, who continued to send money home regularly, ensuring that the family had enough to meet their daily needs.

Nilu, aware of the family dynamics, often felt the strain of these responsibilities. She managed the household chores and took care of everyone while Ramu remained indifferent to the family's struggles. "Ramu Bhaiya focuses only on the shop," Nilu would confide to Dharamveer during his visits. "He doesn't seem to care about the expenses or how we manage at home."

Kedarnath's strict and demanding nature only added to the challenges. Despite Ramu's earnings from the grocery shop, he seldom contributed to the household expenses. Kedarnath frequently pressured Dharamveer for additional money, ignoring the fact that his elder son was also capable of supporting the family. "Dharamveer, we need more money," Kedarnath would say during phone calls, disregarding Ramu's responsibilities.

During this time, Nilu accompanied Dharamveer to Bahaya with their family. The move was necessary to support the reopening of the grocery shop, which had been neglected after Dharamveer joined the army. Nilu's presence helped manage the household, and she played a crucial role in maintaining a semblance of order amid the chaos.

Despite her efforts, Nilu faced significant challenges. Ramu's lack of involvement in household matters and Kedarnath's demanding nature made her life difficult. She was responsible for everything, from cleaning the house to taking care of her younger brothers-in-law. Her days were filled with chores, and she rarely received any appreciation or help.

"It's exhausting, Dharamveer," she would say during his brief visits home. "I manage everything here while Ramu Bhaiya focuses only on the shop. And Baba... he never acknowledges how much I do."

Dharamveer's frustration grew as he saw the strain on Nilu and the imbalance in family responsibilities. He knew that his role as an army man required him to be away, but it pained him to see his wife bearing the brunt of the household duties. Despite these challenges, he continued to provide for the family, sending money regularly and ensuring they had what they needed.

The younger brothers, still in school, were not yet able to contribute financially. Dharamveer's hope was that, in time, they would grow up and be able to share the burden. For now, the responsibility lay heavily on his shoulders.

Dharamveer's dedication to his family was unwavering. He managed to balance his military duties with his responsibilities at home, always ensuring that his loved ones were cared for. He often wondered how different things could be if Ramu took a more active role in supporting the family.

As time passed, Dharamveer continued to fulfill his duties with the same dedication. His love for Nilu and his family kept him going, even during the toughest times. He knew that his sacrifices were not just for his country but also for the well-being of those he loved dearly.

Despite the sadness that enveloped the family after Meera's passing, life had to move on. The villagers and family members comforted themselves with the thought

that perhaps her suffering had ended for the better.
However, for Dharamveer and Nilu, the loss was
profound and enduring.

Meera had been a pillar of sweetness and innocence in
Dharamveer's life. She was his favorite, and he was hers.
They shared a bond that was unspoken yet deeply
understood. Dharamveer often found himself reminiscing
about the times he spent with her, her gentle voice, and
the way she cared for him. "She was always there for
me," he would say to Nilu, his voice tinged with sorrow.
"I miss her so much."

Nilu, too, felt the void left by her mother-in-law's
passing. Meera had been a source of comfort and support,
especially during the challenging early days of her
marriage. Nilu recalled a poignant moment when Meera,
aware of the household dynamics, had offered her a piece
of wisdom wrapped in a blessing. "Let Ramya take all of
your things, just keep quiet. May my son afford and give
you all your desires," Meera had said, her eyes filled with
a mixture of sorrow and hope.

These words stayed with Nilu, a reminder of Meera's
kindness and the silent strength she had imparted. Meera
had understood the struggles Nilu faced and had offered
her a form of solace that Nilu clung to, even after Meera
was gone. Nilu often found herself whispering these
words when times were tough, finding comfort in the
memory of her mother-in-law's gentle encouragement.

In the midst of their grief, Dharamveer remembered the promise he had made to his mother. He had vowed to take care of the entire family and never let them separate. This promise weighed heavily on him, but it was also a driving force behind his unwavering dedication. "I promised her, Nilu," he would say, determination in his eyes. "I promised I would take care of everyone."

Dharamveer continued to send money home, manage the household expenses, and ensure that his siblings were taken care of. He took pride in fulfilling his mother's last wish, even though it often meant sacrificing his own comforts and desires. Every time he felt the weight of responsibility, he remembered Meera's faith in him and found the strength to keep going.

Nilu supported him wholeheartedly. She understood the importance of his promise and shared in his commitment to the family. Despite the challenges, she never complained. Instead, she found ways to keep the memory of Meera alive in their everyday lives, often sharing stories about her with Gopi and the rest of the family. "Your grandmother was a kind and loving woman," she would tell Gopi, her voice filled with warmth. "She cared deeply for all of us."

Together, Dharamveer and Nilu navigated the complexities of their extended family. They managed to create a home filled with love and respect, despite the occasional difficulties with Ramu and the other family members. Their shared memories of Meera served as a source of inspiration and strength, reminding them of the values she had instilled in them.

Even as time passed and the immediate sorrow of Meera's death began to fade, Dharamveer and Nilu never forgot her. They continued to honor her memory by upholding the promises they had made and by nurturing the family she had loved so dearly. Dharamveer's dedication to his mother's last wish and Nilu's unwavering support were testaments to the enduring power of love and family.

Chapter Nine

As the months passed, the sorrow that had enveloped Dharamveer and Nilu slowly began to lift, replaced by a new chapter filled with joy and hope. In March, they were blessed with a beautiful baby girl named Anju. The arrival of Anju brought immense happiness into their lives, providing a source of light and joy amid the challenges they continued to face.

Nilu's heart swelled with love as she held Anju for the first time. "She's perfect, Dharamveer," she whispered, tears of joy streaming down her face. Dharamveer, too, was overwhelmed with emotion, feeling an indescribable connection to his newborn daughter. "She's our little angel," he said softly, kissing Anju's tiny forehead.

The presence of Anju brought new energy to the household. Nilu and Dharamveer's days were filled with the sweet demands of caring for a newborn, and their nights were spent marveling at every little sound and movement Anju made. Her laughter became the soundtrack of their lives, and her innocent eyes brought a sense of peace to their hearts.

One year later, their happiness doubled with the arrival of another daughter, whom they named Ekta. Ekta's birth added another layer of joy and completeness to their family. "We're so blessed," Nilu said, holding both Anju and Ekta close. "Our family is growing, and it's beautiful."

Dharamveer, though often away due to his duties, made every effort to be present for the significant moments in his children's lives. He would come home with gifts, bringing a piece of the world he protected back to his family. "These are for you, my little stars," he would say, handing Anju and Ekta small tokens of his love.

Nilu, with her nurturing spirit, managed the household and took care of their growing family. Her days were busy, filled with the laughter and cries of her children, but she embraced every moment with grace and joy.

"This is what happiness looks like," she often thought, watching her daughters play together.

The family dynamic began to shift with the presence of Anju and Ekta. Ramu and the other family members, though still somewhat distant, couldn't help but be charmed by the innocence and beauty of the two little girls. Even Kedarnath's stern demeanor softened in the presence of his granddaughters. "They remind me of better times," he admitted one evening, watching Anju and Ekta play.

Despite the ongoing responsibilities and the challenges of balancing his military career with his family life, Dharamveer found solace in the love of his daughters. Their smiles and giggles were a reminder of what he was fighting for, and their presence gave him the strength to face any obstacle. "Everything I do is for them," he would tell Nilu, his voice filled with determination.

Nilu's love and support continued to be the backbone of the family. She managed the household with unwavering dedication, ensuring that their daughters grew up in a loving and nurturing environment. Her memories of Meera's wisdom and kindness guided her, and she often found herself channeling her mother-in-law's strength. "I hope I'm making you proud, Ma," she would whisper, feeling Meera's presence in her heart.

The arrival of Anju and Ekta marked a new era for Dharamveer and Nilu. Their lives, once filled with hardship and sorrow, were now overflowing with love and happiness. The challenges they faced only strengthened their bond, and the laughter of their children became a constant reminder of the beauty of life.

As time passed, Dharamveer and Nilu continued to cherish every moment with their daughters. Anju and Ekta grew, their personalities blossoming under the care and love of their parents. The family, despite its complex dynamics and occasional struggles, found joy in the simple moments of togetherness.

As the years passed and the family grew, life continued to evolve for Dharamveer, Nilu, and their children. Their son, Gopi, had been studying in another city, living in a hostel to ensure he received a good education. However, with the arrival of his sisters, Anju and Ekta, Gopi returned home, eager to meet his new siblings and be part of the family's growing love.

Gopi's return was a joyous occasion for everyone. He immediately bonded with
Anju and Ekta, delighting in his role as their protective older brother. "Look, Anju, I got this for you," he would say, presenting his sisters with small gifts and sharing stories of his adventures at the hostel. The girls adored their brother, and the house echoed with their laughter and playful antics.

However, as Gopi grew older, it became clear that the village environment was not conducive to his studies. The distractions and lack of proper educational resources were a concern for both Dharamveer and Nilu. They wanted the best for their son, and ensuring his education was a priority.

After much discussion, it was decided that Gopi would go to live with Dharamveer's sister, who lived in a city with better educational facilities. "It's for your future, Gopi," Dharamveer explained gently. "You need to focus on your studies, and Aunty's place will give you the right environment to do that." Gopi understood, though the decision was bittersweet. He loved his family and the lively household, but he also recognized the importance of his education. "I'll miss you all," he said, hugging Nilu tightly. "But I'll make you proud, I promise."

Dharamveer's sister welcomed Gopi with open arms, providing him with a supportive and structured environment for his studies. Gopi thrived there, excelling in his academics and growing into a responsible and intelligent young man. He often wrote letters to his family, sharing his progress and expressing his love and longing for home. "Dear Ma, I miss you and Anju and Ekta so much. I'm doing well in my studies, and I hope to visit soon."

Back at home, Nilu and Dharamveer missed Gopi dearly, but they took comfort in knowing he was in a better place for his education. Anju and Ekta often asked about their brother, eagerly awaiting his visits. "When will Gopi Bhaiya come home?" Anju would ask, her eyes filled with anticipation. "Soon, my dear," Nilu would reply, holding her close. "He's studying hard, and he'll come home to us soon."

The separation was challenging, but it strengthened the bond between the family members. Dharamveer and Nilu remained dedicated to their children's wellbeing, ensuring that Anju and Ekta received the love and care they needed while Gopi was away. Despite the distance, the family stayed connected through letters and occasional visits, cherishing the moments they spent together.

Dharamveer continued to balance his military duties with his responsibilities at home. His dedication to his family never wavered, and he took pride in the achievements of his children. "We're building a future for them," he would say to Nilu, determination in his eyes. "It's all worth it."

Nilu's support was unwavering, her love for her children and husband guiding her through the challenges. She managed the household with grace, ensuring that Anju and Ekta grew up in a nurturing environment. "We're doing this for them," she would remind herself, finding strength in the love that bound their family together.

Chapter Ten

As the days turned into years, the children grew, and life continued to evolve for Dharamveer and Nilu. Anju, now a bright and curious young girl, began her studies at a nearby school. Her early school years were filled with new experiences and friendships, and she thrived in her studies, much to the delight of her parents.

Recognizing the importance of providing a stable and conducive environment for their children's education, Dharamveer made a significant decision. He secured a quarter in Udhampur, a place known for better living conditions and educational facilities. This move was aimed at ensuring a brighter future for their children, away from the distractions and limitations of village life.

The move to Udhampur was a significant change for the family. Dharamveer took Nilu, Anju, Ekta, and Gopi to their new home, eager to provide them with the opportunities they deserved. The quarter in Udhampur was modest but comfortable, offering the family a sense of security and a better quality of life.

Nilu, ever the resilient and supportive wife, embraced the change with grace. She set up their new home, creating a warm and nurturing environment for her children. "This is a fresh start for us," she would say, arranging their belongings with care. "We'll make the most of it."

Anju and Ekta quickly adapted to their new surroundings. They enrolled in nearby schools and continued their education with enthusiasm. The improved facilities and resources in Udhampur allowed them to explore their interests and excel in their studies. "I love my new school," Anju would tell Nilu, her eyes shining with excitement. "We have so many new things to learn!"

Gopi, though initially hesitant about the move, found his place in Udhampur as well. He continued his studies with dedication, his parents' sacrifices motivating him to do his best. "I want to make you proud, Papa," he would say to Dharamveer, his voice filled with determination.

Life in Udhampur brought new opportunities and challenges. Dharamveer balanced his military duties with his responsibilities at home, ensuring that his family was well-cared for. The move also brought them closer as a family, with more time to spend together and support one another. "We're building a better future for our children," Dharamveer would remind Nilu, his eyes filled with resolve.

The family's new home also became a place of pilgrimage for their relatives. Dharamveer's family members often visited Udhampur to see the famous tirthsthals (pilgrimage sites). These visits brought a sense of connection and tradition, allowing the family to maintain their cultural and spiritual ties. "It's wonderful to have everyone here," Nilu would say, preparing meals for their guests. "It feels like home."

Despite the challenges of balancing their roles, Dharamveer and Nilu managed to create a loving and supportive environment for their children. The move to Udhampur was a turning point in their lives, offering them new opportunities and a better future.

Anju, Ekta, and Gopi flourished in their new home, their lives filled with learning and growth. Dharamveer's dedication to his family and his unwavering commitment to their well-being remained the foundation of their success. Nilu's strength and love continued to guide them, her nurturing spirit creating a haven for her children.

Through the ups and downs, the family remained united, their hearts bound by love and determination. The move to Udhampur was a testament to Dharamveer and Nilu's resilience and their unwavering belief in the importance of family and education. Together, they faced the challenges and embraced the opportunities, creating a future filled with hope and promise

Before the family moved to Udhampur, Nilu and Gopi had shared some precious moments of their lives in different places where Dharamveer was stationed. These memories became a cherished part of their family lore, often recounted with fondness and nostalgia.

In those days, the family moved frequently due to Dharamveer's postings, but Nilu and Gopi always found ways to make each place feel like home. Gopi, being the eldest, often reminisced about those times with his younger sisters, Anju and Ekta.

"Do you remember when we lived in that small town near the border?" Gopi would begin, his eyes twinkling with the light of old memories. "Mama and I were there with Papa before you two were born. It was a tiny place, but it felt like the whole world to me."

Nilu would smile, her heart warming at the recollection. "Those were simple days, but they were filled with so much love and joy. We didn't have much, but we had each other, and that was enough."

Gopi loved to regale Anju and Ekta with stories of his childhood adventures. "I was the cutest kid in the area," he would boast playfully, his sisters giggling in response. "Everyone used to say so! And I had so many friends. We used to run around, climb trees, and play all sorts of games."

One of Gopi's favorite memories was of a festival they celebrated in a small village. "Do you remember, Mama? The whole village came together for the celebration. There were lights, music, and so much food. Papa carried me on his shoulders, and I felt like I was on top of the world."

Nilu nodded, her eyes misty with the sweetness of the memory. "I remember. You were so happy. And your father was so proud. He always tried to make sure we experienced the joy of those moments, no matter where we were."

Dharamveer, too, cherished those memories. He would often join in the storytelling, adding his own perspective. "Gopi was indeed the apple of everyone's eye," he would say, ruffling his son's hair affectionately. "And Nilu, you managed everything so well. Those days were tough, but you always made our little house feel like a home."

Anju and Ekta loved these stories, imagining their brother as a young boy and their parents as a young couple navigating the challenges of military life. "Tell us more, Bhaiya!" they would plead, their eyes wide with fascination.

"Alright, alright," Gopi would say, pretending to think hard. "There was this one time, we were in a place with a big garden. I used to chase butterflies and try to catch them. Mama would laugh and say, 'Let them fly, Gopi.

They're meant to be free.' And I would argue, 'But I just want to hold them for a little while!'"

Nilu laughed at the memory. "You were always so curious and full of energy. It's no wonder you have so many stories to tell."

These shared memories created a tapestry of love and connection that bound the family together. They provided a sense of continuity and belonging, even as life changed and new challenges arose. The stories of their past adventures brought joy to their present and hope for their future.

As they prepared to move to Udhampur, the family carried these cherished memories with them. They were a testament to the love and resilience that defined their lives. Gopi's stories became a bridge between the past and the future, a reminder of the strength and unity that would carry them through whatever lay ahead.

Chapter Eleven

As life continued to unfold for Dharamveer and Nilu, their family experienced significant changes. Both of

Dharamveer's brothers got married, adding new members to the family and further intertwining their lives. However, amidst the celebrations, a tragedy began to loom over Kedarnath's old house, which stood in the middle of the village.

The house, built by Kedarnath's father, had grown old and worn with time. Its age and dilapidation made it difficult to live in, but it was more than just a building; it was a repository of memories and heritage. Despite its state, Kedarnath held onto it dearly. However, his brothers, who had their own plans, began to turn against him. They wanted him out of the house and were becoming increasingly hostile, pressuring him to leave the village.

The conflict reached a boiling point, and Kedarnath found himself cornered. His brothers' actions and demands left him with little choice, and the situation became untenable. Dharamveer, despite the challenges he already faced, knew he had to step in and protect his father.

"We can't let them force him out," Dharamveer said to Nilu, his voice filled with determination. "This house means a lot to him, and to us. We need to find a solution."

With a heavy heart, Dharamveer decided to build a small room at the entrance of the village. It wasn't much, but it would provide Kedarnath with a place to live without the constant threat from his brothers. "It's not the same as the old house, but it's safe," Dharamveer explained to his father. "You'll be at peace here."

Kedarnath reluctantly agreed, recognizing the necessity of the move. He appreciated Dharamveer's efforts and understood the sacrifices being made. "Thank you, my son," Kedarnath said, his voice tinged with both gratitude and sorrow. "I know this isn't easy."

The new arrangement also meant that Dharamveer's younger brother, who had gotten married after him, would live in the small room with the younger brother and Kedarnath. This living situation was far from ideal, but it was a compromise that allowed the family to stay together while providing some measure of safety and stability.

Despite the challenges, Dharamveer's actions were a testament to his unwavering commitment to his family. He worked tirelessly to ensure that his father and brothers had a place to live, even if it meant making personal sacrifices. "We have to take care of each other," he would often say to Nilu, his resolve unwavering. "Family comes first."

Nilu supported Dharamveer through this difficult time, managing their household and caring for their children with love and dedication. She understood the weight of

Dharamveer's responsibilities and stood by his side, offering strength and encouragement. "We'll get through this together," she assured him, her voice filled with unwavering faith.

The move to the new room at the village entrance marked a significant shift for Kedarnath and the family. While it wasn't the home they had known and cherished, it was a place of safety and refuge. Dharamveer's actions reinforced the family's bond, reminding them of the importance of unity and support in the face of adversity.

As the family settled into their new living arrangements, they continued to navigate the complexities of their lives. The challenges were many, but so were the moments of joy and connection. Through it all, Dharamveer's dedication to his family never wavered, and Nilu's love and support remained a constant source of strength.

Together, they faced each day with resilience and hope, knowing that as long as they had each other, they could overcome any obstacle. The family's journey was a testament to the power of love, unity, and the unwavering commitment to those they held dear.

As time went on and through careful savings and hard work, Dharamveer managed to finance the reconstruction of the old house, transforming it into a beautiful, spacious home. Though he was stationed far from his hometown, his younger brothers oversaw the construction, ensuring the project went smoothly. The house, now a symbol of the family's resilience and unity, stood proudly in the village, a testament to their collective efforts.

Chapter Twelve

However, just as things seemed to be settling into a harmonious routine, a new challenge emerged. The youngest brother, after his marriage, developed troubling habits. He began inhaling cigarettes and drugs and drinking beer excessively. His condition quickly deteriorated, causing great concern among the family members.

When Dharamveer learned of his brother's struggles, he knew he had to act. He couldn't bear to see his brother's life spiral out of control. "We have to help him,"

Dharamveer said to Nilu, worry etched across his face. "He's our responsibility, and we can't let him destroy his life."

Determined to help his brother overcome his addictions, Dharamveer decided to bring him to the city where they were currently living. He hoped that a change of environment and closer supervision would help steer him away from his destructive habits.

Nilu supported Dharamveer's decision wholeheartedly. "It's the right thing to do," she agreed. "We'll take care of him and help him get back on his feet."

Dharamveer arranged for his youngest brother to come to the city, welcoming him into their home with open arms. "You're not alone," Dharamveer told him firmly. "We're here for you, and we're going to get through this together."

The initial days were tough. Dharamveer's brother struggled with withdrawal symptoms and cravings, and it took all of Dharamveer's and Nilu's patience and support to help him stay on the path to recovery. They enrolled him in a rehabilitation program, attended counseling sessions with him, and made sure he was surrounded by a supportive environment.

"You can do this," Dharamveer would often say, encouraging his brother. "We believe in you."

Nilu played a crucial role in this period, providing a nurturing and stable environment at home. She prepared nutritious meals, offered emotional support, and ensured that their household remained a haven of positivity and hope. "We're a family," she would remind her brother-in-law gently. "And families take care of each other."

Slowly but surely, Dharamveer's brother began to show signs of improvement. The change of environment, coupled with the relentless support from Dharamveer and Nilu, started to make a difference. He began to regain his strength and health, showing glimpses of the person he used to be before addiction took hold.

Throughout this period, the rest of the family also rallied around Dharamveer's brother. His siblings, both near and far, offered their support and encouragement. "Stay strong," they would say during their visits and phone calls. "We're all rooting for you."

The journey was far from easy, but with each passing day, Dharamveer's brother grew stronger, more determined to rebuild his life. Dharamveer's unwavering dedication to his family, despite his own demanding responsibilities, shone through, inspiring everyone around him.

Eventually, Dharamveer's brother was able to overcome his addictions. It was a hard-won victory, achieved through love, support, and sheer determination.

Dharamveer's decision to bring his brother to the city had been the turning point, providing the necessary intervention that saved his brother's life.

The family, now even more united after overcoming this challenge, celebrated the transformation. They knew that while there would always be challenges ahead, their bond and commitment to each other would help them face anything that came their way.

Dharamveer's dedication to his family, both immediate and extended, remained a beacon of strength. His actions demonstrated the true meaning of family, showing that with love and support, even the most difficult challenges could be overcome. And through it all, Nilu's unwavering support and care ensured that their home remained a sanctuary of love and hope for everyone.

After overcoming his addiction, Dharamveer's youngest brother, Raj, managed to secure a job in the city. Raj's recovery and newfound stability were sources of great relief and joy for the entire family. Raj had a daughter and a son, and his family joined Dharamveer's household in the city.

Raj's children were still young and lively, and their presence, while joyous, created a bustling and often noisy environment. This proved challenging for Dharamveer's own children, who needed a quiet space for their studies. Despite the disruption, Dharamveer and Nilu welcomed

Raj's family with open arms. They understood the importance of supporting Raj during this critical phase of his recovery and reestablishing his life.

"We're family," Dharamveer reminded Nilu and their children. "We need to help them until they can get back on their feet."

Nilu, ever the nurturing and accommodating presence, managed the household with patience and grace. She found ways to balance the needs of everyone, ensuring that her children had the necessary quiet time for their studies while also tending to the needs of Raj's young children. "It's temporary," she would say reassuringly to her children. "Let's make the best of it and help them as much as we can."

Raj, grateful for the support, was determined to show his appreciation and respect for his brother's generosity. He worked hard at his new job and made a conscious effort to maintain his sobriety. "I owe you everything," Raj often told Dharamveer. "Thank you for believing in me and giving me this chance."

Despite the challenges, the combined families found ways to create joyful moments together. The children, though sometimes disrupted, formed close bonds and enjoyed each other's company. Laughter and play filled the house, reminding everyone of the importance of family.

Eventually, Raj reached a point where he felt confident and stable enough to move back to their hometown with his family. "I've left those dark days behind," Raj told Dharamveer, his voice filled with gratitude and determination. "It's time for us to return home and start anew."

The day Raj's family prepared to leave was filled with mixed emotions. Nilu packed them food for the journey, her eyes misty with the thought of their departure. Dharamveer's children, though relieved to regain their quiet study environment, hugged their cousins tightly, promising to visit soon.

"We'll miss you," Anju said, holding Raj's daughter close. "Take care and come back to visit."

Dharamveer stood by Raj, his hand on his shoulder. "You've done well," he said, pride evident in his voice. "Continue to stay strong and build a good life for your family."

Raj nodded, his eyes shining with gratitude. "I couldn't have done it without you. Thank you, Bhai."

As Raj's family left for their hometown, Dharamveer and Nilu watched them go, their hearts filled with a sense of fulfillment. They had supported their family through a difficult time and helped them find a path to a better future. The house, once bustling with noise and activity, returned to a quieter state, allowing Dharamveer's children to focus on their studies.

Life in Udhampur continued with a renewed sense of peace and accomplishment. The family had faced numerous challenges, but each one had strengthened their bonds and reinforced their commitment to each other. Dharamveer and Nilu's unwavering support and love had seen them through the toughest times, and their home remained a sanctuary of warmth and hope.

The future looked promising, filled with the potential for new achievements and happiness. And through it all, the family's unity and dedication to one another would continue to be their greatest strength.

A few months after Raj and his family had returned to their hometown,
Dharamveer received a devastating phone call. The news was heart-wrenching: Raj had passed away due to severe lung cancer. The shock and sorrow that gripped Dharamveer were overwhelming. Raj had always been his favorite brother, the one who had shown unwavering respect and obedience. The loss felt insurmountable.

Dharamveer's world seemed to shatter at that moment. He had worked so hard to help Raj recover and build a better life, only for it to end so tragically. Nilu, sensing the depth of her husband's pain, immediately began preparing for their journey back to the village. "We need to be there for the family," she said softly, her voice filled with compassion and resolve. "Raj needs us one last time."

They packed quickly, and Dharamveer, Nilu, and their children made the journey back to the village. The usually vibrant and bustling household was now enveloped in a pall of grief. Raj's wife and children were inconsolable, their tears reflecting the profound sense of loss that permeated the air.

Dharamveer took charge of the funeral arrangements, ensuring that every detail was handled with care and respect. Despite his own heartache, he knew he needed to be strong for his family. "We'll give him the farewell he deserves," he told Nilu, his voice steady despite the pain in his eyes.

The funeral was a solemn affair, attended by friends, family, and villagers who had known Raj. Dharamveer performed the rites with a heavy heart, his mind flooded with memories of his beloved brother. "I'll always remember you, Raj," he whispered during the final rites. "You were more than a brother—you were my friend, my confidant. I promise to take care of your family."

Nilu stood by his side, offering silent support. She knew how much Raj had meant to Dharamveer and shared in his grief. Their children, though young, understood the gravity of the situation and stayed close to their parents, offering their own small gestures of comfort.

After the funeral, Dharamveer made sure all the expenses were taken care of, ensuring that Raj's wife and children were not burdened by financial worries during such a difficult time. "We're here for you," he assured Raj's widow. "You'll always be part of our family, and we'll support you in any way we can."

In the days following the funeral, Dharamveer spent time with Raj's family, helping them navigate their grief and plan for the future. He made arrangements for Raj's children's education and ensured that his widow had the necessary support to manage her household. "We'll get through this together," he said, his voice filled with determination. "Raj would want us to stay strong and take care of each other."

Returning to Udhampur was bittersweet. Dharamveer carried the weight of his brother's loss with him, but he also found solace in the love and support of his family. Nilu and their children were his anchors, providing comfort and strength as they adjusted to life without Raj.

As time passed, Dharamveer continued to honor Raj's memory by staying true to his promise. He regularly visited Raj's family, offering support and guidance. His dedication to his family remained unwavering, a testament to his character and the deep bonds of love that defined their lives.

The family's resilience was a beacon of hope, demonstrating that even in the face of profound loss, they could find a way to move forward together. Through it all, Dharamveer's commitment to his loved ones never faltered, and Nilu's unwavering support ensured that their home remained a sanctuary of love and healing.

Chapter Thirteen

As days turned into months and then years, Raj's children grew up, and the question of managing expenses and their education became increasingly pressing. Raj's wife, although resilient, faced significant challenges in providing for her family. This situation underscored the importance of women being selfreliant and capable of standing on their own feet.

Fortunately, Raj had owned a small shop in Bahaya, which he occasionally opened and managed before his passing. Dharamveer decided to put the shop to good use, renting it out to generate a steady income for Raj's widow. The rental income from the shop provided a modest but crucial financial support, allowing Raj's wife to manage her household expenses.

"We'll use the shop's income wisely," Dharamveer advised her. "It will help with daily expenses, but we need to ensure the children's education is taken care of too."

Taking on the responsibility of his brother's children's education, Dharamveer made sure that they had the resources they needed to succeed. He paid for their school fees, bought their books and uniforms, and ensured they had everything required to focus on their studies. "Education is the key to their future," he often said. "We must do everything we can to give them a strong foundation."

Raj's children, inspired by their uncle's dedication and hard work, studied diligently, understanding the sacrifices being made for them. They knew that their education was a priority and that it was a way to honor their father's memory. Dharamveer's unwavering support became a beacon of hope and stability in their lives.

Nilu, as always, played an integral role in this process. She frequently visited Raj's family, offering emotional support and practical help. She helped Raj's widow manage the household and guided her on budgeting the shop's income effectively. "You're not alone," Nilu would remind her gently. "We're all in this together, and we'll make sure the children have a bright future."

Dharamveer's commitment to his extended family did not waver, even as he balanced his responsibilities in the army and his own household. His dedication to Raj's children was a testament to his love for his brother and his belief in the importance of family. "Raj would have done the same for my children," he told
Nilu one evening. "It's our duty to support them."

Over time, the shop's income and Dharamveer's financial assistance ensured that Raj's family remained stable. The children excelled in their studies, motivated by their uncle's faith in their abilities and the opportunities provided to them. Dharamveer's support extended beyond finances; he also took an active interest in their academic progress and personal growth.

The family's resilience and unity were evident in how they navigated this challenging period. Raj's widow, with

Nilu's guidance, learned to manage the shop's income efficiently, gradually becoming more confident and self-reliant. The children, fueled by their uncle's unwavering belief in them, worked hard and aspired to achieve great things.

Dharamveer's actions demonstrated the profound impact of familial support and the importance of standing by loved ones in times of need. His commitment to Raj's family was a powerful reminder of the strength that comes from unity and the enduring bonds of love and responsibility.

As the years passed, Raj's children grew into accomplished individuals, their success a testament to the sacrifices and support provided by Dharamveer and Nilu. The family's journey was a poignant example of resilience, love, and the unbreakable bonds that held them together through life's trials and triumphs.

Dharamveer's younger brother, despite his efforts, struggled to find stable employment. He moved from one city to another, constantly searching for better job opportunities. Each time he secured a new job prospect, he turned to Dharamveer for financial assistance. "Bhaiya, whenever you lend me money, my job prospects always turn out positive," he would say with a hopeful smile.

Dharamveer, understanding the pressures his brother faced and wanting to support him, often provided the necessary funds. "We're family," Dharamveer would say. "It's my duty to help you, especially when you're trying to improve your situation."

The younger brother's family, which included his wife, a daughter, and a son, remained in the village. They lived modestly, relying on the support that Dharamveer provided. Nilu, ever the pillar of support, often sent them care packages, ensuring they had essential items and some comforts from their extended family.

"It's tough for them," Nilu remarked one evening as she packed another box of supplies. "But we must keep supporting them until they find stability." Dharamveer nodded, his thoughts weighed by the constant demands. "I just hope he finds a steady job soon. It's not easy managing everything, but family comes first."

Despite his busy schedule and the financial strain, Dharamveer never hesitated to help his younger brother. Each time he sent money, he hoped it would be the turning point that would finally bring stability to his brother's life. He knew the importance of a stable job, especially with a family to support.

In the village, the younger brother's wife managed their household and took care of their children. The daughter and son attended the local school, and although their lifestyle was simple, they were surrounded by a supportive extended family. Dharamveer and Nilu made sure that the children had everything they needed for their education.

"We're grateful for everything you've done," the younger brother would often say during his visits to Dharamveer's home. "I'll repay your kindness once I'm settled."

"Just focus on getting stable work," Dharamveer would reply. "That's the best way to repay me. Make sure your family is well taken care of."

The cycle of job searching, moving, and seeking financial help continued, but Dharamveer never lost faith in his brother. He understood the difficulties of finding stable employment and remained a constant source of support and encouragement.

Nilu, with her nurturing nature, often provided emotional support to her sisterin-law and the children. "You're doing your best," she would tell her during their conversations. "Things will get better, and we're here to help you through this."

Through it all, Dharamveer and Nilu's household remained a beacon of hope and stability for the extended family. They balanced their own responsibilities while ensuring that their loved ones had the support they needed. Their actions demonstrated the true essence of family: unwavering support, love, and a commitment to each other's well-being.

Over time, the younger brother continued to search for a stable job, buoyed by the knowledge that his family stood by him. The financial support and encouragement from Dharamveer played a crucial role in keeping his hopes alive. And while the road was challenging, the bonds of family and the strength of their unity carried them through the toughest times.

Chapter Fourteen

As the years of Dharamveer's service drew to a close, he decided to shift his family to a city where they could live on rent. This move was aimed at ensuring better educational opportunities for his children. It was a significant transition, but one that Dharamveer felt was necessary for their future.

During this time, an unexpected and challenging situation arose. Vishesh, Dharamveer's younger brother, had a son who began exhibiting alarming behavior. The boy was often uncontrollable, throwing things and acting stubbornly without any apparent reason. After several consultations, doctors diagnosed him with a severe inner brain condition that caused these outbursts.

Understanding the gravity of the situation, Dharamveer immediately stepped in. He knew that his brother's family needed more support than they could manage alone. "Bring him to our rental house in the city," Dharamveer told Vishesh.
"Nilu will take care of him, and we'll get him the medical attention he needs."

Vishesh, overwhelmed and grateful, agreed. The family moved the boy to Dharamveer's home. Nilu, ever compassionate and resourceful, embraced the responsibility without hesitation. She rearranged their schedule and routines to accommodate the new challenges that came with caring for her nephew.

"We'll manage," Nilu reassured Dharamveer. "He needs us, and we'll do whatever it takes to help him."

Dharamveer provided financial support, covering the medical expenses and ensuring that the boy had access to the best possible care. He instructed Nilu to take him to the hospital for regular check-ups and treatments. "He's our family," Dharamveer reminded her. "We'll do everything we can."

The days were long and often difficult. The boy's unpredictable behavior required constant vigilance and care. Nilu, with her nurturing nature, managed to create a stable environment for him. She patiently dealt with his outbursts and took him to his medical appointments, often spending long hours in the hospital.

Dharamveer, although busy with his duties, remained deeply involved. He would call Nilu frequently to check on the boy's progress and offer his support. "How is he today?" Dharamveer would ask. "Is there anything more we can do?"

Slowly, with consistent medical treatment and the loving care provided by Nilu, the boy's condition began to stabilize. The outbursts became less frequent, and he started showing signs of improvement. The doctors were optimistic, crediting the dedicated care he received at home for his progress.

Nilu's tireless efforts did not go unnoticed. Vishesh, deeply moved by his brother and sister-in-law's support, expressed his gratitude repeatedly. "I don't know how to thank you both," Vishesh said, tears in his eyes. "You've done more than I could ever ask for."

"We're family," Nilu would respond, her voice filled with warmth. "We take care of each other, no matter what."

As time passed, the boy's condition continued to improve. The stability and care provided by Dharamveer and Nilu played a crucial role in his recovery. The experience, though challenging, brought the family even closer together. It reinforced the bonds of love and support that had always been the cornerstone of their relationships.

Dharamveer's unwavering dedication to his family, even as his service years were ending, was a testament to his character. He balanced his responsibilities with grace, ensuring that his loved ones were always taken care of. The sacrifices he and Nilu made were driven by their deep sense of duty and love for their family.

As the years of service ended and Dharamveer transitioned to civilian life, the lessons learned and the bonds strengthened during these times remained a guiding light for the entire family. The story of how they navigated these challenges together would be a source of inspiration and pride for generations to come.

The last years of Dharamveer's army service were particularly grueling. He was posted in a remote and inhospitable area, where severe cold made survival a daily struggle. The harsh weather conditions were relentless, with temperatures plunging to dangerous lows. The soldiers had to endure these extreme conditions while performing their duties, often with little more than a few hours of sleep each night.

The physical and emotional toll was immense. Each day was a test of endurance and resilience. The soldiers, including Dharamveer, faced these challenges with unwavering commitment, knowing that their service was vital for the security and well-being of their country. The isolation and harsh conditions made it difficult to stay connected with their loved ones, and the constant vigilance required to perform their duties left little room for rest or relaxation.

Despite the hardships, Dharamveer took immense pride in his service. He understood the significance of his role and the sacrifices involved. Whenever he had the chance, he would share stories of his experiences with his children. He spoke about the harsh winters, the long hours, and the camaraderie among the soldiers. "It was tough, but we knew we were doing something important," he would say, his voice filled with pride. "We were there to protect our country and our people."

When Dharamveer finally returned home, the sense of relief and joy was overwhelming. The comfort of his home, the warmth of his family, and the ability to sleep in a cozy bed were sources of immense satisfaction. The transition from the harsh conditions of the remote area to the comforts of home was a profound contrast, and Dharamveer savored every moment of it.

He would often recount his experiences to his children with a mix of nostalgia and pride. "There were days when the cold was so intense it felt like it would cut through you," he would describe. "But we made it through, because we were all in it together. And when we finally came home, it felt like we had achieved something truly special."

His stories were not just about the difficulties he faced, but also about the sense of accomplishment and the pride he felt in serving his country. "Every struggle, every cold night, was worth it for the chance to serve and protect," he would tell them. "I hope you understand the value of dedication and sacrifice."

The experiences Dharamveer shared with his family not only highlighted the challenges of his service but also underscored the pride and honor he felt in being part of something larger than himself. His children listened with rapt attention, absorbing the lessons of resilience, commitment, and patriotism that came with their father's stories.

As he settled back into civilian life, Dharamveer continued to cherish the moments with his family and the newfound comforts of home. His service had shaped him in profound ways, and the pride he took in his contributions remained a defining part of his identity. The sacrifices he made and the hardships he endured were a testament to his dedication, and his stories of perseverance and pride served as a powerful reminder of the true value of service

Chapter Fifteen

After serving his country for 22 years, Dharamveer finally returned to his hometown, a milestone that filled him with a profound sense of accomplishment and relief. The transition from the rigorous demands of military life to the calm of civilian life was a significant change, but one that Dharamveer welcomed with open arms.

His family had settled in a small town, just 5 kilometers away from his hometown. Despite the proximity, Dharamveer chose to live in rental rooms in the small town with his family while frequently visiting his village. His love for his village remained strong, and he cherished every opportunity to reconnect with his roots.

The decision to live in the small town was practical, allowing his children to attend better schools and providing his family with more amenities. However, Dharamveer never lost touch with his village, frequently making the short trip back to visit. His presence in the village was a source of joy and pride for the locals, who had always admired his dedication and service.

The first thing Dharamveer did upon his retirement was to honor a promise he had made to his eldest sister,

Vidya. She had asked him that if he returned home safely and retired soon, he would renovate the village temple, which stood at the entrance of the village. The temple, though small and weathered, held significant cultural and spiritual importance for the community.

True to his word, Dharamveer set about fulfilling Vidya's request. He began planning the renovation with meticulous care, ensuring that every detail was attended to. "This temple has been a cornerstone of our community," Dharamveer said. "It deserves to be preserved and celebrated."

The renovation project was more than just a restoration; it was a labor of love. Dharamveer oversaw the work personally, ensuring that the temple was refurbished with respect and attention to its historical and cultural significance. He coordinated with local craftsmen and volunteers, and the project became a community effort.

The transformation was remarkable. The temple's entrance was revamped, and its interiors were cleaned and beautifully decorated. Dharamveer made sure to incorporate traditional elements while also modernizing certain aspects to make it more functional and welcoming. The project not only restored the physical structure but also rejuvenated the spiritual essence of the temple.

The reopening of the temple was celebrated with great enthusiasm. Villagers, old and young, gathered to witness the revitalized temple and express their gratitude to Dharamveer. The renovation not only honored his promise but also symbolized his deep connection to his roots and his commitment to his community.

"Thank you, Dharamveer," Vidya said with tears in her eyes as she admired the completed temple. "You've fulfilled your promise, and you've given our village a precious gift."

Dharamveer smiled, his heart swelling with pride and contentment. "It was my honor," he replied. "This temple is a part of our heritage. It's a place where we come together as a community, and it was important to me that it be preserved for future generations."

As Dharamveer continued to balance his time between his small-town home and his village, he felt a deep sense of fulfillment. His retirement was marked by both personal and communal achievements, and the renovation of the temple was a testament to his enduring love for his village and his dedication to preserving its legacy.

A few weeks after settling into his retirement, Dharamveer decided to treat himself and his younger brother to a new motorcycle. It was a symbol of the freedom and joy he was now able to experience after years of dedicated service. The motorcycle became a cherished possession, not just for the convenience it provided but for the adventures it promised.

Dharamveer, always thoughtful, also considered his brothers in his plans. After a year of managing his retirement funds wisely, he made another significant purchase: a four-wheeler. The vehicle was more than just a mode of transportation; it was a means to bring the family together and create lasting memories.

With the new car, Dharamveer organized family outings that became highlights of their lives. The entire family of four brothers and their wives would gather for rides, exploring nearby towns and scenic spots. Each journey was filled with laughter and stories, rekindling the bonds that had been strengthened over the years.

One of the most cherished outings was when they all traveled to their mother's house. The trip was a nostalgic return to their roots, where they reminisced about their childhood and celebrated their mother's legacy. The presence of the four-wheeler made it easier to transport the entire family and the items they brought along, including gifts and supplies.

The car also facilitated regular visits to important family gatherings and events. Whether it was attending festivals, family functions, or simply enjoying a day out together, the vehicle played a crucial role in maintaining close-knit family connections.

Dharamveer, always one to appreciate the simple joys of life, often reflected on how these moments brought him immense happiness. "It's not just about the vehicle," he would say. "It's about the time we spend together, the memories we create, and the joy of being able to share these experiences with the people I love."

The motorcycle and the car became symbols of the new chapter in Dharamveer's life—a chapter filled with family, freedom, and the simple pleasures of togetherness. The journeys they took and the memories they made were a testament to the bonds of family and the fulfillment that came with enjoying the fruits of a long and dedicated career.

Chapter Sixteen

When the pandemic struck, it brought unexpected challenges and disruptions to everyone's lives. Dharamveer and his family were no exception. With restrictions and uncertainties surrounding them, they decided to relocate to their village to ensure a safer and more stable environment during these trying times.

Despite the upheaval, Dharamveer found solace in being able to live with his entire family once again. After decades of separation and frequent travel due to his army service, the opportunity to spend extended time with his loved ones in the village was a source of great joy for him. It was a chance to reconnect with his roots and strengthen familial bonds.

However, the relocation also posed significant concerns, particularly regarding the education of his children. Dharamveer was determined to ensure that his children's education did not suffer due to the move. He was resolute in finding solutions that would provide them with the best possible opportunities despite the challenging circumstances.

For his older children, Anju and Gopi, Dharamveer had a clear plan. "Anju and Gopi will continue their studies at

Banaras Hindu University (BHU)," he decided. "We'll make sure they have the resources they need to pursue their education there." BHU, being a prestigious institution, offered a range of academic programs and had a reputation for providing quality education. Dharamveer's decision reflected his commitment to maintaining their educational standards.

Gopi and Anju were both relieved and motivated by their father's determination. "We're grateful for the support and opportunities you're providing us," Gopi said. "We'll do our best to make the most of it."

For Ekta, the youngest of the three children, Dharamveer sought a solution closer to home. "Ekta will be admitted to a nearby good school," he said. "We want to ensure she receives a quality education while we're living in the village."

Finding a suitable school for Ekta was crucial to ensuring her continued academic growth. Dharamveer and Nilu researched and visited local schools to find one that met their standards. They chose a school known for its strong academic program and supportive environment, ensuring that Ekta would thrive in her studies.

As the pandemic continued to affect daily life, Dharamveer and his family adjusted to their new routine. They embraced the time spent together in the village, finding comfort in their shared experiences and the simple pleasures of rural life. The village, with its slower pace and close-knit community, provided a sense of stability and connection that was particularly valuable during uncertain times.

Dharamveer's proactive approach to his children's education, coupled with his ability to adapt to the changing circumstances, highlighted his dedication to his family's well-being. The challenges posed by the pandemic were met with resilience and a commitment to ensuring that his children's futures remained bright.

Despite the difficulties, the time spent in the village became a period of growth and rediscovery for Dharamveer and his family. The bonds they strengthened and the experiences they shared during this time would become cherished memories, reflecting the enduring strength and unity of their family.

Chapter Seventeen

As Dharamveer settled back into village life, he was confronted with a troubling revelation that shook the foundation of his long-held perceptions about his family. The once familiar and comforting village life now seemed overshadowed by a complex web of familial dynamics and financial disputes.

Upon his return, Dharamveer discovered that his younger brother, Vishesh, who had always been favored by their father, was at the center of the family's financial issues. Vishesh had been entrusted with managing the money from the fields that had been rented out to other farmers. This arrangement had been set up by their father, Kedarnath, who had shown a clear preference for Vishesh throughout his life.

It soon became apparent that Vishesh had been less than transparent about the management of these funds. Dharamveer found that Vishesh was not only receiving the income from the fields but was also frequently asking for more money from Dharamveer to cover personal expenses. The situation was exacerbated by Vishesh's tendency to live beyond his means, creating a constant financial strain on Dharamveer.

To make matters worse, Dharamveer learned that the fields he had purchased early in his military career, which had been bought in the name of his father as a gesture of respect and duty, were now being demanded by Vishesh. Vishesh was adamant that the fields be distributed among the siblings, including himself, despite the fact that Dharamveer had made these purchases with the intention of supporting his family and securing their future.

The double-faced nature of Vishesh's behavior was disheartening. Despite the support and financial help Dharamveer had provided over the years, Vishesh's actions seemed driven by greed and a lack of gratitude. Dharamveer felt betrayed and conflicted, torn between his desire to uphold family unity and the need to address the financial mismanagement and entitlement displayed by Vishesh.

Dharamveer's attempts to resolve the situation were met with resistance and hostility. Vishesh, backed by the favoritism of their late father, was unwilling to acknowledge the contributions and sacrifices Dharamveer had made. The family tensions came to a head as Dharamveer struggled to maintain a balance between supporting his family and protecting his own interests.

Despite the challenges, Dharamveer remained committed to his principles. He continued to provide financial support where necessary, but he also took steps to address the mismanagement of funds and ensure that his contributions were used appropriately. He sought legal and financial advice to protect his investments and to prevent further exploitation by Vishesh.

The situation tested Dharamveer's resilience and patience. His deep sense of duty and commitment to his family was now at odds with the reality of dealing with a family member who was more interested in personal gain than in mutual respect and cooperation.

Through this tumultuous period, Dharamveer's actions were guided by a desire to do what was right, even when it meant confronting uncomfortable truths and navigating complex family dynamics. He faced the difficult task of redefining his relationship with Vishesh and ensuring that his own sacrifices and contributions were recognized and respected.

Ultimately, the experience highlighted the complexities of family relationships and the challenges of managing expectations and responsibilities within a family framework. Dharamveer's journey through these issues was a testament to his strength of character and his unwavering commitment to his values, even in the face of adversity.

As Dharamveer continued to live in the village, he uncovered a disturbing reality about the family he had always been dedicated to. The outwardly sweet and innocent facade of his relatives began to crack, revealing a different side that was far from what he had imagined. His relentless efforts to support and assist his family, both financially and emotionally, seemed to have only highlighted their underlying resentment and entitlement.

Despite his sacrifices, Dharamveer discovered that many of his relatives harbored negative thoughts and ill feelings towards him. Their demeanor had shifted, revealing a more calculating and ungrateful attitude. This was particularly evident when Dharamveer, after years of generous support, began to cut back on his financial contributions due to the strain of his own resources and the mismanagement by Vishesh.

He was taken aback by how quickly their demeanor changed once they felt that his financial support was not as abundant as before. Dharamveer's realization was a harsh one, filled with disillusionment and sadness. The very family members who had once appeared to be in dire need of his help were now expressing disdain and dissatisfaction, questioning his ability to assist them and showing no respect for the sacrifices he had made.

One relative, in a moment of unguarded honesty, remarked, "He doesn't have a regular salary. We can't count on him for our financial needs." This comment stung deeply. It was a stark contrast to the appreciation and respect Dharamveer had expected, given the countless times he had gone above and beyond to support them.

Another relative expressed frustration, saying, "When he was helping, it was all good. Now that he's not, it's like he doesn't care about us anymore." The accusation was particularly hurtful, as it completely disregarded the genuine concern and effort Dharamveer had put into supporting his family.

Dharamveer's heart ached as he reflected on these sentiments. The experience left him feeling:

- **Disillusioned**: "I gave my all, expecting nothing in return, only to find that my family sees my help as a given rather than a gesture of love and sacrifice."
- **Betrayed**: "It's painful to realize that the same people I supported unconditionally now view me with resentment and suspicion when I need to step back."
- **Sad**: "Serving your family and fulfilling their desires without seeking anything back is supposed to be a noble act, but when it's met with disrespect and ingratitude, it feels like a betrayal."

The experience underscored a painful truth: while Dharamveer had always acted out of love and duty, the lack of reciprocity and respect from his family members was deeply disheartening. It became clear that his support was taken for granted, and that once the flow of financial aid slowed, the true nature of some family members was revealed.

Despite the bitterness of the situation, Dharamveer's resolve remained strong.
He continued to act with integrity and kindness, even in the face of ingratitude. His actions were driven by a sense

of duty and a desire to uphold his values, rather than seeking validation or recognition from others.

The experience taught Dharamveer a valuable lesson about the complexities of family dynamics and the nature of unconditional support. It highlighted the importance of setting boundaries and managing expectations, even when it comes to loved ones.

The months that followed were some of the hardest in Dharamveer's life. The initial relief of being back in his village and reconnecting with his family had given way to a painful reality. The very family he had tirelessly supported now seemed to be entangled in their own issues and misgivings, creating a rift between them.

The tension came to a head when it was time to divide the lands and property left by their father, Kedarnath. Dharamveer, who had always put family first and sacrificed his own comfort for their well-being, now found himself on the receiving end of decisions that seemed to disregard his contributions and sacrifices.

The division of the property was conducted with a cold efficiency that stung deeply. Dharamveer was allotted a small piece of land on the outskirts of the old family home—a stark contrast to the more substantial portions given to his brothers. The decision was a blow to Dharamveer, who had envisioned a future where he could build a home for his family in the village he loved.

The reality of the situation hit hard: the home he had started to build for his family would not be his to keep. The sense of displacement and the unfairness of the arrangement weighed heavily on him. He was faced with the task of constructing a new home on the small piece of land allocated to him.

Undeterred, Dharamveer set about creating a new place for his family. With a heavy heart but unwavering resolve, he secured a home loan and began the process of building a modest 2BHK house on the small plot of land. It was a far cry from the family home he had hoped to build, but it was a testament to his determination and commitment to providing for his wife and children.

The new house, while small, represented a new beginning. It was constructed with love and care, reflecting Dharamveer's dedication to his family despite the challenges he faced. The process was arduous, and every step of the way was marred by the sense of loss and betrayal, but Dharamveer persevered.

As he worked on the house, he often reflected on the painful irony of the situation. Despite all the sacrifices he had made for his family, the outcome was a small, modest home rather than the legacy he had hoped to leave. The new home was a symbol of both his resilience and the harsh reality of familial expectations and disappointments.

His children and wife supported him through this difficult period, understanding the sacrifices and hardships involved. They knew that the new home was more than just a physical structure; it was a testament to their father's unwavering love and dedication.

In the end, Dharamveer's new house was completed, and while it was smaller than he had envisioned, it became a place of refuge and family warmth. Despite the injustices and heartache he faced, he took pride in the fact that he had managed to create a home for his family amidst adversity.

The experience was a powerful reminder of the complexities of family relationships and the often-unseen sacrifices made in the name of love and duty. Dharamveer's story was one of enduring strength and resilience, marked by a willingness to face hardship with courage and a commitment to his family, no matter the cost.

The unfolding events added another layer of distress to Dharamveer's already turbulent life. The division of the property and land, which had initially left him with a small plot and a sense of disillusionment, was compounded by a further blow that left him feeling deeply hurt and betrayed.

The shops in Bahaya, which had once been a significant asset for the family, were divided among the siblings.

Dharamveer had envisioned using his share to open a jewelry shop with his youngest brother, Raj, in the hope of building a new business venture. This dream was particularly important to him, as it represented not just an opportunity for financial stability, but also a chance to create something positive amidst the turmoil.

However, while Dharamveer was away visiting his wife's mother, the family proceeded to divide the shops without his consent or input. The division was conducted hastily and with a lack of consideration for Dharamveer's plans and contributions. The shops were divided into four equal parts, but the process was marred by a clear disregard for fairness and respect.

To Dharamveer's dismay, the area he was allocated was not only the worst of the four, but also smaller than his original share. The division seemed to be less about equitable distribution and more about disadvantaging him further. The hurtful reality of the situation was exacerbated by the fact that the decision was made while he was absent, leaving him with little recourse to voice his concerns or negotiate a fair share.

The news struck him with profound sadness and frustration. His vision of starting a jewelry shop and contributing to his family's financial stability was dashed. The new area he was given was not conducive to establishing a successful business, and his dreams of building something meaningful seemed to crumble before his eyes.

Dharamveer felt a deep sense of betrayal, realizing that his family's actions were driven by a lack of respect and consideration for his contributions and aspirations. The division of the shops was a stark reminder of the underlying negativity and selfishness that had surfaced within his family.

In his own words, Dharamveer reflected on the situation with a heavy heart:

- **"To give away what you've worked for and dreamt of, without even a moment of consideration for your plans, is a bitter pill to swallow. It's as if my sacrifices and hopes were just shadows in the eyes of those who should have understood my struggles."**
- **"When you give your all, expecting that love and respect will be reciprocated, only to find that your efforts are met with disregard, it feels like a betrayal that cuts deeper than any material loss."**
- **"The division of the shops was not just about property; it was a reflection of the disregard for my dreams and the years I spent supporting this family. The smallest piece of land, the worst shop – it all symbolizes a larger disregard for everything I've done."**

Despite the sting of these actions, Dharamveer remained resilient. He chose to focus on the positives, drawing strength from his family and the support he received from his wife and children. They rallied around him, understanding the depth of his hurt and providing him with the emotional support needed to navigate through these challenging times.

Dharamveer's journey through these trials was marked by unwavering perseverance and a commitment to maintaining his dignity and integrity. He continued to work towards creating a stable and loving environment for his family, even as he grappled with the pain of being sidelined and underestimated by those he had always supported.

Chapter Nineteen

The division and betrayal that Dharamveer experienced left deep scars, but the most painful revelation came with the behavior of his younger brother, Vishesh. The once-promising younger sibling had veered off into a path that was both dangerous and morally corrupt. Vishesh, who had once been the recipient of Dharamveer's love and support, was now deeply entrenched in illegal activities—selling harmful substances to the youth of the community.

As Vishesh's involvement in these activities grew, so did his wealth, which only served to amplify his ego and attitude. The money and the illicit power it brought began to transform Vishesh into someone unrecognizable to Dharamveer, who had always seen him as a younger brother to guide and support.

Despite the deep sense of betrayal and hurt, Dharamveer tried to approach Vishesh with a sense of brotherly concern. He hoped to guide Vishesh back to a righteous path, believing that with some intervention, his brother could still turn his life around. Dharamveer's intentions were driven by genuine concern for Vishesh's future and the well-being of the community affected by his actions.

However, Vishesh's response was nothing short of shocking and deeply painful. Rather than appreciating his brother's intervention, Vishesh reacted with hostility and aggression. He accused Dharamveer of jealousy and of trying to undermine his success, which was an affront to Dharamveer's sense of fairness and brotherly love. Vishesh's newfound wealth had inflated his ego to such an extent that he openly belittled Dharamveer, even resorting to physical violence against him.

This confrontation was a heart-wrenching experience for Dharamveer. The very brother he had nurtured and supported was now an embodiment of everything he stood against. Vishesh's behavior was a stark contrast to the values Dharamveer had tried to instill and the love he had always shown.

Dharamveer felt a profound sense of loss and disillusionment. His brother's actions and attitude were not only a personal betrayal but also a blow to the principles he had dedicated his life to upholding. The situation left Dharamveer with a mixture of emotions:

- **Heartbreak:** "To see someone I loved and cared for so deeply fall into a path of destruction and disrespect is more painful than any material loss. It's a betrayal that cuts to the core of my heart."

- **Disillusionment:** "When you've given your all to someone, only to be met with hostility and arrogance, it shakes your faith in the values you hold dear. It's a reminder of how easily love can be overshadowed by greed and corruption."

- **Frustration:** "I tried to help him, to guide him away from the harm he was causing. Instead of gratitude, I faced accusations and violence. It's a bitter pill to swallow when your efforts to save someone are met with such animosity."

Despite the crushing weight of this betrayal, Dharamveer remained steadfast in his values. He chose to distance himself from Vishesh's toxic influence, focusing instead on maintaining his own integrity and continuing to provide for his family through his legitimate business endeavors.

The family's dynamics had shifted dramatically, with each member pursuing their own path, largely detached from one another. Dharamveer's resilience and commitment to his principles were tested in ways he had never anticipated. His story became one of enduring heartbreak and steadfast determination, illustrating the complexities of familial relationships and the challenges of maintaining one's values in the face of deep-seated betrayal and adversity.

Dharmveer's enduring love for his family, despite the betrayals and hardships, highlights a remarkable aspect of his character. Even after the deep hurt and the numerous challenges he faced, he continues to hold a special place in his heart for them. His dedication to family is evident in his efforts to be present at their celebrations—attending birthdays, anniversaries, and other significant events. His presence at these occasions reflects a sincere desire to remain connected and supportive, regardless of past grievances.

Nilu's perspective on the situation adds another layer of resilience and optimism to their story. She firmly believes in the principle of cosmic justice: that the good they have done will eventually come back to them in a positive form, while the negative actions directed toward them will ultimately have repercussions for those who committed them. This belief provides Nilu with a sense of peace and acceptance, allowing her to navigate the difficulties with grace.

Together, Dharmveer and Nilu embody a spirit of enduring hope and unconditional love. Their ability to maintain their integrity and support each other through trials demonstrates a profound strength and commitment to their values. Despite the challenges they face, their story remains one of perseverance, resilience, and an unwavering belief in the goodness of their actions and intentions

Dharmveer and Nilu's experience underscores a profound sense of disillusionment and heartbreak. Despite their unwavering dedication and the sacrifices they made for their family, they faced betrayal and disrespect. Their journey reflects a deep and painful realization:

- **"We gave our all, expecting nothing in return but respect and genuine care. Instead, we were met with betrayal from those we loved and supported the most. The depth of our commitment was met with disregard, and it's a bitter truth we had to face."**

The expectation of respect and understanding, rather than material gain or reciprocation, highlights their pure intentions and the sincerity of their efforts. The betrayal they faced was not just a personal loss but a shattering of the trust and values they held dear.

- **"To realize that the very people we cared for and sacrificed so much for could turn against us, it's a wound that cuts deep. Our intentions were never about receiving anything back, only about upholding our values and supporting our loved ones. Yet, what we received in return was a painful lesson in human nature and betrayal."**

This disillusionment is a harsh contrast to the love and dedication they had always shown. It reveals the stark difference between their selfless actions and the actions of those who failed to appreciate their sacrifices.

- **"We thought our actions and love would be met with respect and gratitude. Instead, we were**

met with betrayal, and that realization is a painful truth we have to accept. The respect and care we hoped for were replaced with actions that contradicted everything we believed in."

Despite the hurt, Dharmveer and Nilu's resilience shines through. Their ability to continue supporting their family, attending important events, and maintaining their values in the face of betrayal is a testament to their strength and character. Their story remains a poignant reminder of the complexities of familial relationships and the challenges of maintaining integrity amidst adversity.

Were We Wrong" is a poignant, reality-based story that delves into the profound challenges faced by an army man after retirement. Written with deep empathy and insight, the book sheds light on the often overlooked struggles of those who have dedicated their lives to serving their country. The narrative, while featuring imagined names and places, is rooted in the real-life experiences of the author's father, maternal uncles, and her mom's dad and uncle, all of whom served in the army, as well as her better half. Through the story of Dharmveer, the author aims to reveal the harsh realities and emotional turmoil that many soldiers endure when they return to civilian life. This heartfelt account not only honors the sacrifices made by these brave individuals but also exposes the unexpected betrayals and societal challenges they face, offering readers a sobering glimpse into the true cost of service and the resilience required to navigate life after the uniform is hung up.

Acknowledgments

First and foremost, I would like to express my deepest gratitude to the brave men and women of the armed forces, whose sacrifices and dedication inspire us all. This book is a tribute to their unwavering commitment and resilience.

To my father, maternal uncles, and mom's dad and uncle—your stories, strength, and perseverance have been the guiding force behind this book. Your experiences have provided a window into the real-life challenges faced by soldiers, both during and after their service.

A special thank you to my better half, whose own journey in the army has given me invaluable insights and a profound appreciation for the sacrifices made by military families. Your support and encouragement have been a pillar of strength throughout the writing process.

I would also like to extend my heartfelt thanks to my family and friends for their unwavering support and understanding as I embarked on this journey. Your belief in me has been a constant source of motivation.

To my editors and publishers, thank you for believing in this story and for your guidance in bringing it to life. Your expertise and dedication have been instrumental in shaping this book.

Finally, to the readers, thank you for taking the time to delve into the realities faced by our servicemen and women. It is my hope that this book provides a deeper understanding and appreciation of their sacrifices and the complexities they face upon returning to civilian life.

With gratitude,

[ANJALI SINGH]

About The Author

ANJALI SINGH grew up in Kharouni, Bihar, and now lives in baxur. She is pursuing her graduation from Banaras Hindu University with B.A. She is daughter of Dharmendra Kr. Singh and married to Vinay Kr. Singh. Shieldmaidens Destiny is her first book. Visit her online with minefeat on any platform.

9 7 9 8 8 9 5 1 9 4 2 2 5